SHERLOCK HOLMES: THE CRYPTID FILES
THE CASE OF MOTHMAN

N.S. THORNGRAVE

ISBN 979-8-9931564-1-5

Trigger Warning Menu

Dear Reader,

Please note that the story you are about to read has dark undertones. There are a variety of topics that will make some people uncomfortable and other people smile. Please review this list of trigger warnings and read with caution.

Consider yourself warned.

Master & Slave

Asphyxiation

Masks

Murder

Sexual Harassment

Blood

Guns

Gun Shots

Mouth Gag

Anal Sex

Anal Oral Sex

Monster Sex

Semen

Choking

Vampires

Age Gap Troupe

Chains

Death

Darkness

Oral Sex

Violence

Blindfolding

Corpses

Terms: Slut & Whore

Masturbation

Biting

Anal Orgasm

Unique Peen

Wings

Fangs

Spit

Drug Use

Missing Persons

Whipping

Female Ejaculation

Gore

Acknowledgments

I want to thank my wife for always supporting me and helping make these stories a reality, as well as for her assistance with editing this book. I want to thank my brother, KT, for his assistance with the book cover design. To my family and friends, who may be disturbed by reading my stories, you're welcome. I also dedicate this book to Thor, who will always be my fur baby. Finally, to my readers, those monster smut-loving baddies who love the dark, the taboo, and the downright sexy, this book is for you.

Prologue

The leaves crunched underneath his black boots. He was now in the woods, deep within the part of the forest where the whispers of a civilized world disappeared, and the sounds of the natural earth began to bellow. The crisp night air was invigorating as he drew a deep breath through his nose and exhaled through his mouth. The journey to get here was long, with days spent on ships, trains, and an Oldsmobile, which brought him within walking distance to the woods… to his woods.

Vlad was from Romania; he had lived there for a very long time, but alas, like most creatures, change is inevitable. Though he was known by many names in his time on this Earth, Vlad was his preferred title, for now. He longed for something more, so he researched a new destination. A place he went to where he could shed his skin and be reborn as something different, something more primal than he had been before. Now in the woods of Point Pleasant, West Virginia, he found his new home. Vlad removed his gray suit coat and tossed it on the ground a few feet away from him.

The coat hit the forest floor, startling a moth that fluttered toward Vlad. He extended his gloved finger, and the moth landed as if it were the most natural thing to do.

Vlad stared at the moth and brought it up to his mouth. He curled his pink lips open, exposing his razor-sharp canine fangs, and ate the moth.

Within seconds, Vlad stumbled in pain and fell to his knees. He opened his mouth as he made a hacking noise as if he were choking. His spine heaved up and down; his hands tore through both his gloves as he sank his now-clawed, gray hands into the black soil beneath him. Next were his feet, ripping through the black boots, sending the soles ricocheting and hitting a tree. His feet turned into a set of talons with blade-like claws. Then came the wings, both ripping through the back of his suit and expanding from side to side. The wings were leathery, charcoal gray, and dripping with blood at the end of them after emerging from Vlad's skin.

Vlad's face, shrouded by moth wings, hid what remained of his former self. His eyes gleamed a bright, fiery red—like the light you see only when staring into the depths of hell and despair. The moth wings on his face fell flatly to the ground, revealing a grayish leather hide that replaced the fragile human skin he once adorned.

He stood up and looked at his claws. He expanded his wings in and out. The red eyes glowed as they scanned the forest around him. He now knew the transformation was complete; long gone was Vlad the Romanian vampire, now there was only a half-man, half-moth…Mothman.

Chapter 1

A few months have passed since the great detective Sherlock Holmes arrived in Twain, Georgia, and moved into a quaint office on the Bedford Farm. The small, modest cabin was payment to Sherlock for traveling to the U.S. to investigate the case of a curious beast terrorizing a property. In exchange for his keen investigative skills, Myra Bedford gave Sherlock a sliver of a parcel of land from her acreage. It was a convenient place for Sherlock to call his temporary home while he investigated cases in the U.S. Not just any case, though: Sherlock was interested in folklore, monsters, and the occult.

His companion, Thor, a rotund dachshund and trusted ally, enjoyed the new environment and seemed to make himself at home in the southern setting. Myra Bedford lived on her farm with her son and had a companion who lived in the woods. Companion was a better word than beast.

Sherlock enjoyed his time getting acquainted with the town. Though he was still very much seen as an outsider in this small rural community, he wanted people wondering things about him and starting rumors of how he was actually dating Myra Bedford, which was not true but was better than everyone in town finding out Myra's genuine love interest was Skookum, an 8 foot tall beast covered in hair with the strength of an army and the intuition of jackrabbit.

Sherlock's partner, Dr. Watson, was investigating his own cases in their London branch. They would often communicate by phone and letters to keep each other informed about the cases they were working on. It was an arrangement that worked out well for both Sherlock and Watson.

Sherlock was always on the lookout for his next case, though no one case seemed to be that odd enough to him or in the realm he desired to dive into. Sherlock knew that if a beast like Skookum existed, there had to be more creatures lurking in the shadows and feeding on their existence. Skookum was the name of a beast he thought only existed in lore. Though it was his first case in the United States, Sherlock quickly discovered that the legend of Skookum was not a myth but instead an intriguing account of a large primate stalking the mountainous terrain of North America.

Sherlock would travel to the local library, where Carmina, the librarian, would save for him articles from around the United States about curious and unexplained happenings. He enjoyed his time at the library and the small talk with Carmina. She always seemed to give him articles that she felt were worth investigating. On his last visit, she gave him three articles. He did not read it at the moment because the weather was turning for the worse, and he wanted to be back in his office before the southern wind and rain would create hazardous road conditions. He hitched a ride back to the Bedform Farm with three carefully curated newspaper articles. He knew that this would be his nightly read for the moment; he just hoped there was something in those stories that was worth investigating.

Chapter 2

Watson had been dealing with internal struggles for months. He became involved in a secret organization of witches and mysterious figures, La Lechuza, which had members worldwide and held influential positions. The leader of this outfit was none other than Carmen, the local librarian in London. After Watson began researching the meaning of certain symbols, Carmen took notice and made it clear, in a brutal way, that he was not to dig any deeper into information about La Lechuza.

Watson now found himself as an associate of the organization in return for certain favors that only La Lechuza could provide. Though it was clear, Carmen oversaw the organization of La Lechuza and Watson. Sherlock was to know nothing of this arrangement, which was part of the deal Watson had made with Carmen. It was also a way to keep Sherlock safe. Sometimes the less someone knows, the better.

The doorbell buzzed outside Watson's office. He slowly made his way to it and turned the brass door handle to reveal Carmen standing on the other side.

"Dr. Watson, what a pleasure to see you yet again."

Watson was not surprised by her presence; he had expected her, in fact. After she placed a call to him, asking him to murder someone in the same town that Sherlock was in.

"Carmen, please do come in. I was somewhat expecting you."

Carmen smiled and walked in. Watson was still taken aback by her beauty; she had these eyes that stared deep into your bones. If gothic allure was ever sexy, she wore that aura with every fiber of her being.

"Well, it is always nice to be expected, Watson. Do not worry, I am here on business. The business of our arrangement. After all, you wanted information, I gave it to you."

Watson was annoyed because he knew Carmen had him under her spell, not a trance, but the kind of spell that only a woman like her could intoxicate others with — her intrigue.

Carmen walked towards the fireplace located on the far wall of his office and stood in front of it. The fireplace logs ignited and began burning as if the flames had been burning for hours. It was a trick of hers that she used before, one that Watson still found impressive to this day.

"Have a seat, Watson."

Watson walked over to the armchair that Sherlock typically sat in and made himself comfortable.

"Watson, you asked me some time ago if the Ripper of London was really locked away in the Tower of London. You wanted to know if you and Sherlock caught the right man. Of course, you didn't, and now you know that thanks to me."

"Yes, I recall, and you seem to think I am forever indebted to you because of it."

His tone was sarcastic but carried the edge of confidence as well.

"I brought you into La Lechuza organization after you practically begged me, don't be an ingrate."

"You owe me a favor, and it is time to pay that favor. You will be going to Twain, Georgia, and killing a man by the name of Ripshaw. Of course, that isn't his real name, just a guise so no one gets suspicious."

Watson took a deep breath as he felt the heat from the fireplace keep a part of his cheek warm.

"Why do you want me to kill an innocent man? I am not capable of cold-blooded murder, even if you do command it."

Carmen walked over to Watson and kneeled in front of him. She grabbed her hands and placed one on each of his thighs. She pushed his legs open. Watson squirmed but enjoyed the feel of her hands over his trousers as she rubbed them back and forth.

"He is not innocent and hardly a man, Watson. He is another former associate of La Lechuza. We know him as the Plague Doctor, and he has done damage, too much damage; now he must go."

Watson felt uneasy. Carmen's hand kept moving slowly up and down his legs; he felt frozen, partly in fear and partly in arousal.

"You see, the Plague Doctor got his name because he would blend special illnesses for our organization. Illnesses that we would use to eliminate those that needed to be gone in a way that would not lead to speculation of something other than someone who got sick."

"How do you even find someone who would create illnesses?"

Watson, being the true detective that he is, could never hide his curiosity.

"He isn't the original Plague Doctor, of course, but his family line certainly is. His family used to poison rats and set them free in the streets of London with deadly illnesses."

"As per usual, I had to come in and clean up his family's mess, but the family trait of creating illnesses became generational."

"Clean up their mess? You mean you are responsible for the Great Fire of London?"

"Well, in truth, we were already getting the plague under control. The fire put an end to it even more quickly. I never said I was responsible."

Carmen smiled a toothy grin at Watson.

Watson moved his arm from the armchair and placed it over Carmen's right hand to stop her from moving it up and down his leg.

"How will I live with myself if I do this?"

Carmen clawed her long, black fingernails down Watson's pant legs.

"How will you live with yourself if you don't?"

She asked him quizzically. Then Carmen stood up.

"It has been decided, Watson, do not worry, I will be traveling with you, except that I have business in another part of North America. However, we will be taking a flight together, La Lechuza will cover the cost of this and all expenditures."

"What the hell am I supposed to tell Sherlock, Carmen? Don't you think he is going to wonder why I am in the United States?"

Watson was scrambling, trying to find any reason to talk his way out of traveling and killing another person.

"You will tell Sherlock you are there for a case you are working on. You will not give him the details. Once you finish your assignment, you can help Sherlock with whatever he is working on."

Watson was reluctant, but he seemed to have no alternative. He could have said no and kept fighting, but he didn't want to. The truth is, he enjoyed Carmen telling him what to do and commanding him. Carmen knew he enjoyed it as well.

She walked towards the door as it flung open automatically. She turned to Watson and smiled with those lips that made men lose concentration.

"We leave in three days, buy yourself a new pair of trousers by then, Watson."

Carmen turned back towards the door and walked out. The moment her body left the threshold, the fireplace flames extinguished cold.

Watson stood up and looked down to see scratch marks on his pants, and they were shredded into rags. Another gift from Carmen, another way to let Watson know that she is the dominant one in their relationship.

Chapter 3

The baby-blue Chevy Bel-Air cruised slowly along the wooded roads in Point Pleasant, West Virginia. The driver was a hot-headed college sophomore named Brian East, the local football town hero with a cannon for an arm and brown wavy hair. Brian was a spoiled brat. Teachers would look the other way if he failed a class or committed one of his obnoxious pranks in high school. Brian got everything he ever wanted; his parents treated him as if he were made of gold, and undoubtedly, in their eyes, he was.

The only thing Brian never got but wanted was sitting right next to him. Laney Fiora Martino. She was not the most popular girl when she attended high school; she wore glasses and had bigger bones than the other girls. She was a bookworm and kept to herself, and dabbled in the occult. She was the absolute opposite of Brian. She found herself in his car after he asked her out one day when he saw her sitting alone at a picnic table outside the community college they now attended. Of course, he asked her out when no one was around. He told her she could not tell anyone he was taking her out.

"Laney, maybe you and I should go out and have a good time."

Laney was so surprised and caught off guard by the fact that he was caressing her hair and even interested in her.

She nodded in agreement. Now they were cruising down the road to some place he told her he liked to hang out.

"You sure are driving fast. How often do you come out here?"

Laney looked at the pine trees lining the road as Brian zoomed his car down the highway. She was nervous; here she was with the former high school football star who asked her out, and she didn't know how to act. He would never have asked her out when they were in high school, but now that she is a freshman in college, Brian sees Laney as another notch on his belt.

"I come out here every so often, it's a good place to have some privacy if you know what I mean?"

Brian placed his hand on Laney's thick thigh, but she said nothing. He just kept looking out the window, figuring out what to do and how to do it.

The truth was Brian wasn't that interested in Laney at all. He figured that because other guys ignored her, she would be an easy score. An additional name for the girls in the school who had gotten into the back seat with their legs in the air.

Brian slowed as the Chevy's headlights turned on a wood path into the forest, shining on the pine trees at night.

"Where are we going?"

Laney knew the answer; she knew what was expected of her from Brian. She didn't know whether she would go through with it. Having sex for the first time was not on her to-do list this week; on the other hand, he was handsome and muscular.

"Like I said, a private spot so you and I can get to know each other better."

He slid his hand higher on her thigh. He appreciated how soft her skin felt, and he figured the closer he could get to her groin, the more she could get used to the idea of putting out some ass tonight.

Brian made a few more turns in the woods, and Laney was utterly lost as to where they were in the forest.

The Chevy pulled to a slow stop, and Brian turned off the engine and the headlights.

Laney knew what was expected of her. She was a freshman in college, had already turned nineteen years old, and was still a virgin. Something she was semi-proud of, but she did have urges and wanted to get laid. She heard whispers from other girls when she was in high school who were the same age and had gone all the way. The thought that she could release some of those sexual urges with the strong and popular guy seemed like a good option, like any other.

"Slide a little closer to me, Laney."

Laney complied and slid closer. Brian placed his hand on her cheek, turned her face, and began kissing her. Laney had never kissed anyone before with tongue, but it seemed natural to her, and she enjoyed it. Her body was releasing some of the tension she was feeling on the drive.

Brian moved from kissing her lips to kissing and eventually sucking on her neck. She leaned her head back and placed her hand behind his head, running her fingers up his hair. A sound escaped her mouth, and it was a melting moan.

Then Laney heard a thud.

"Brian, did you hear that? I heard something outside."

The spoiled football star was not paying attention to what she was saying; he knew she was putty in his hands.

Brian moved his hand over her big, round breasts and then began unbuttoning her blouse. She ignored what she heard before; she was back in the zone of her sexual exploit. Her blouse was now unbuttoned.

"Take off your top, baby."

Brian commanded, and Laney took a breath, then took off her white blouse and placed it on the seat beside her.

Without Brian asking, Laney unclasped her pink laced bra in the back and took it off, bringing a huge smile to his face.

"You have amazing tits!" This made her smile, a guy paying attention to her body.

Brian kissed down her chest. When he got to her nipple that was darker than he thought it would be, it slipped it right into his mouth as he began sucking on her tits, first on one and then the other. She moaned again, loving how it felt, then her concentration was snapped again out of the moment.

Laney heard another thud, this time louder and closer.

"Brian, wait, there is something out there. I heard another noise."

Brian raised his head and looked out the car window as quickly as he could so he could get back to action with Laney.

"There is nothing out here; we are alone, trust me. Now, where were we?"

Brian leaned back in his chair and began unbuckling his pants. He took his dick out and fully expected Laney to suck on it.

Laney was hesitant; it was the first time she had seen a penis before, in all honesty, though she enjoyed the view of seeing a male body part, Brian's penis seemed relatively thin and small.

"Come on, Laney, bring your head down."

Brian placed his hand on the back of her head and started bringing her head down, but before she could get close enough to even whisper at his cock, something hit the car.

"What the fuck was that?!"

Laney popped her head back up and looked around, now nervous and instantly scared.

Brian was mad; he was seconds away from getting a blow job, and now something killed the mood.

"I told you there was something out there."

Laney was aggravated that Brian hadn't listened before.

Then something caught both their eyes: it was massive and in front of the car. A creature like something out of a horror film. Its thighs were muscular, and its groin was covered with black feathers. The arms glistened in the moonlight, and its eyes glowed red.

"Holy shit!" Brian had a sensation he was not used to; it wasn't being horny; it was being scared.

Laney froze as her breasts were still hanging out in full view of whatever this creature was.

* *

"My, what a lovely delight in front of me. Two human bodies ripe for the devouring." The Mothman could feel their pulses racing, their hearts practically beating out of their chests.

He took a moment to stare at the girl through the window, ignoring the male who was cowering behind the steering wheel.

To flex his attributes, the Mothman expanded his tattered wings and bared his fangs that had the sharpness of an ice pick.

Mothman's eyes focused on Laney, and he could not stop looking at her; he was mesmerized by her plump breasts and soft-looking skin.

"Let's see how to get into that vehicle." The Mothman licked his lips, and a snake tongue came out, which Laney noticed; it scared her even more.

Mothman moved closer to the vehicle, his gaze fixated on Laney's succulent flesh.

"Let's see how good their reflexes are."

He ran towards the vehicle and jumped right before he reached the hood, into the air. They did not hear him land.

"This tree branch should give me enough height to create enough of a scare to get them out of that car."

SLAM!

Mothman landed on the Chevy; he could hear the screams from inside the car. Then he jumped down to the passenger side. His groin was level with the passenger window, and Laney looked over at the grouping of feathers that covered the creature's midsection.

"Ahh, there we go, the boy has begun to cry. The girl, however, keeps looking out; her pulse is racing, and I can feel her blood vibrating as it speeds through her veins. But she is still looking at me."

Laney looked over to see Brian crying out of fear. Something about his sobbing was very unattractive. In that instance, she no longer saw the high school star; she saw a scared boy with an unimpressive penis.

Mothman stepped back to get a better look at Laney. She turned and looked out the window at him, her breasts still on full display.

Mothman was aroused by looking at her, something he typically did not feel when viewing his victims.

The feathers covering his groin parted, and out slid his cock, emerging from the feathers. Laney took notice that the winged creature's penis was four times the length of Brian's and thick. At the end of the shaft, his penis split into two. His penis had two cock heads at the end of it, separated by a few inches from one another. The creature's dick matched the split of his snake-like tongue. It was gray and slick. Though Laney took in every part of this feature, she was still petrified looking at the creature.

"I think it's time I have a taste of this girl, even if I have to rip the door open to do it."

As he approached the vehicle, Laney knew she had to do something; her date was useless.

"Brian, turn on the car and drive!" She screamed at him as loud as she could, but it was no use; he had his hands on his face and was encapsulated by fear.

Laney slapped Brian hard across his face.

"Turn on the fucking car, you idiot!"

Brian complied as the Mothman placed his clawed hands on the passenger-side window.

The car engine roared to life.

"Put it in reverse!"

Laney had no patience with Brian's cowardice. She grabbed the shifter and slammed it into reverse, then she slammed her saddle shoe on top of Brian's foot that was placed on the gas pedal. The car began moving backwards quickly, which was enough to snap Brian out of his scared trance and start driving out of the forest.

"Leaving so soon, are they? Well, let's give them a little chase."

As the Chevy was going in reverse, Brian found a spot to spin the car around and speed towards the main road. The moment the car was on the highway, Laney looked into the side mirror and saw the creature flying behind them at high speed. It looked like a massive gray bullet was zipping right in their direction.

"Hurry up! It's following us!"

Laney looked back. The creature was gone, or so she thought. A tap on her passenger-side window made her look to her right, where the beast was right next to her window. She screamed a startled yelp.

She looked right into his red, glowing eyes and was entranced. Fear began to subside slowly. She couldn't explain it, but she saw a human in his eyes.

"Time to slow down and let them go, I've vision bonded with her. She will find her way back to me."

The Chevy continued down the highway. Brian and Laney stayed quiet the whole ride back to town. Once they were safe, Laney put on her pink lace bra and button-down blouse again. She looked at the rearview mirror, adjusted her hair, and fixed her glasses.

Brian pulled up to Laney's house and didn't even put the car in park.

"Brian, are you okay?" She asked as she placed her hand on his arm, and he quickly jerked it away.

"I'm fine! Listen, Laney, don't you tell anyone what happened out there. If you do, I will tell everyone at the college you are the biggest slut and practically begged me for it."

His tone was defiant. Laney knew Brian's threat was to cover up the fact that he didn't want people to know he was a coward, that he cried like an infant at the first sign of trouble.

"Brian, that's not true, you know it!"

"Yeah, whatever, a few more minutes in the woods, and you would have been bent over in the back seat. Keep your mouth shut, or I swear everyone will know you are easy. Who do you think they will believe, you or me?

Laney was furious; she saved both their asses, and he was trying to shame her into lying. That was the last straw for the night.

"You tell anyone I am a slut, and I will tell everyone we did go all the way and that you have a small dick. I will tell them I couldn't even find it, you piece of shit."

When Brian looked over at Laney, he did not have enough time to react to the full fist that was coming towards his face. Making contact with his nose, he started bleeding all over his white T-shirt and his car as the blood flowed out of his face like a fountain.

"That is the most satisfying thing that has happened to me all night!" Laney screamed at the now bloody Brian.

Laney got out of the car and slammed the door as she stomped towards her house. She could hear Brian grumbling in the background, more than likely crying again.

When she walked into her house, she passed her aunt Monica, who was watching television on the couch.

"How was your night, Laney?"

"I don't want to talk about it, but I promise you there will not be a second date."

Laney's aunt nodded; she knew that with Laney's mother gone, it was a fine line she had to toe between friend, aunt, and guardian. She knew she would hear more about it when Laney was in the mood to talk.

As the bedroom door slammed closed. She dropped onto her bed face-first; she was absolutely exhausted from her wild night out.

Chapter 4

Sherlock sat down on the wooden chair in his small office that also served as his cabin. The table was rustic and had seen better days, undoubtedly a piece to be admired in its prime. His accommodation was modest but fitting for the rural environment. His companion, Thor, was nestled asleep on the green wool blanket that was on the bed.

Sherlock grabbed the three newspaper articles Carmina had given him and began reading. He was not hopeful that his following case would be in this stack, but alas, he decided they might be worth reading, even if only for the entertainment value of the stories.

The first newspaper was from Wisconsin, the title of the article read:

"The Beast of Bray Road"

"Well, that's an interesting title indeed. What do you think, Thor?"

Sherlock knew Thor was asleep and turned to look at him.

Thor snored loudly and shuffled his back paw; other than that, he was not waking up for anyone.

"Very astute of you, Thor. I'll give it a read out loud for both of us. Never say I don't read you bedtime stories."

Now that Sherlock was done with his sarcasm for his furry friend, he began to read the article.

"The small community is on alert today as the Beast of Bray Road has appeared once again. This account is even more terrifying than the last. A man, who wished to remain anonymous, was driving down Bray Road a week ago and reported that, around midnight, a large beast sprang up from next to the road. Thinking it was a person in distress, the driver slowed only to see what appeared to be a 7-foot-tall wolf standing on its hind legs. The snot was covered in blood as what looked to be a piece of raw meat was hanging from its glistening teeth. The beast then began to move towards the car as the driver sped off. The driver was so terrified that he went home and told his wife what had occurred. Though no police report was filed, his wife encouraged him to reach out to our gazette to run the story as a warning to those who drive by Bray Road to be careful, especially if you are traveling at night."

"Hmmm, the case does have intrigue, though having an eyewitness that may not want to speak to me would make the case a gamble. Let's put this one down as a maybe, Thor."

The following article hailed from Puerto Rico with reports stretching across Texas.

"El Chupacabra Destroys Farming Community" was the title of the following story.

Sherlock cleared his throat, took a sip of his hot tea that he made, and relit his marijuana cigarette before reading again. Though a cannabis user in England, he made a contact in town who also enjoyed partaking in Earth's natural elements and could always get him a supply when he asked for it, for a premium price, of course.

He then began to read the following article out loud, for Thor's enjoyment, clearly and not because Sherlock was going mad.

"Farmers in the small city of Canóvanas have reported waking up to dead livestock. This situation began a few weeks ago, when a man by the name of Pedro Romus stated to local police that someone killed his chickens. Initial reports state that the chickens were drained of all their blood, and bite marks were visible on the animals. A neighbor of Mr. Rumos also reported a dead goat, drained of all its blood. The night before he made the discovery, he saw two glowing eyes behind a tree near the goat pen. He stated it looked as if someone was dressed in a dark green goblin costume. Initially thinking it was someone pulling a prank on him, he now believes this goat-sucking creature is no human at all. Several other accounts have had similar situations with dead livestock around their properties. The town named the creature El Chupacabra, which translates to "Goat Sucker".

In the Rio Grande Valley of Texas, several farmers reported similar phenomena to those in Puerto Rico. One witness in Texas stated that they saw the creature, which appeared to be a mutant-looking dog with grayish-green skin, no hair, and the teeth of a large coyote. The investigation is ongoing in Puerto Rico and in Texas.

"Well, now, that is interesting. However, the logistics of traveling between Puerto Rico and

Texas while Watson is in London did not seem ideal. Our resources would be too spread too thin."

"On to the next one, Thor, and by the way, have I told you that your help has been invaluable in the search for our next case?"

Sherlock looked over at Thor, who was sound asleep and still very much snoring.

The following article and the last one he received were from the city of Louisville, Kentucky.

"Man Claims Pope Lick Monster Hypnotized Him!"

"A man in Louisville has claimed that the famed creature, the Pope Lick Monster, hypnotized him. Dan Fenderson was sitting on his porch one late afternoon, and a creature he described as half-man, half-goat approached his property from the dense woods. Dan ran inside, grabbed his rifle, and pointed his gun at the creature. Mr. Fenderson states he does not recall what happened next, other than he heard the voice of his deceased wife echoing from this goat man. He claims to have entered a state of trance and was frozen. Next thing he knew, he woke up on his back, lying on his porch with his rifle nowhere to be found. Locals claim Mr. Fenderson is a well-known alcoholic, and his descriptions of events are nothing more than an alcohol-induced hallucination. Still, some citizens in the town are on high alert for the Pope Lick Monster."

"Wonderful Thor, a mysterious account from a drunk. I've heard better stories in my days. This one will be tinder for the fire."

Sherlock was frustrated. Though two out of the three cases were very interesting to him, he was still not convinced any of them were worthy of his attention.

In the distance, Sherlock heard the moans of Skookum, or as he affectionately called him, Bigfoot. Skookum was having his nightly sexual appetite satisfied by Myra Bedford, the owner of the farm, and based on the sound Sherlock heard nightly, she was doing a fantastic job at keeping Bigfoot satisfied.

Sherlock finished his tea and placed what was left of his cannabis cigarette on the amber glass ashtray. It was time for Sherlock to get some rest and begin his search tomorrow, yet again, for another case.

Chapter 5

Watson and Carmen arrived safely at Atlanta airport. Though Watson traveled with a suitcase, Carmen did not.

"Watson, I have arranged a ride for you to get to Twain, Georgia. You should be there in a few hours."

Carmen reached into her luxurious breasts and pulled out a small piece of paper that was folded up. She handed the parchment note to Watson.

"What is this? Your last will?" The sarcasm flowed out of Watson like a waterfall.

Carmen smiled, put her hands around Watson's neck as if she was giving him a long hug goodbye. She whispered seductively in Watson's ear.

"The note has the location of the Plague Doctor. How you kill him is up to you. First visit Sherlock and let him know you are just passing through."

Carmen bit the bottom of Watson's ear, and he slowly closed his eyes in a brief moment of relaxation.

"Carmen, one of these days, I am going to bite back."

Carmen removed her hands from around Watson and took a step back.

"Good boy." Carmen smiled, patted Watson on the cheek, and turned around and began walking away.

Watson didn't need to bother asking her how she would know he killed Ripshaw; La Lechuza had eyes everywhere.

With that, Watson turned around and walked out of one of the terminal exits at the airport. Only to find a man with a vest standing outside of a pickup truck holding a sign that read "Watson".

"Hello, I'm Dr. Watson. You must be my transport."

"That I am Dr. Watson, hop in the truck, we have a long ride."

Something about this man seemed familiar, his voice perhaps.

"Do I know you? I have an odd feeling we have spoken before."

The man smiled and nodded.

"Indeed, you have. I am the one who picked up your friend Sherlock from the train station when he came to Georgia a few months ago. The name is Ripshaw."

Watson paused momentarily. What did Carmen do? Is the man transporting Watson the same man he had to kill?

As Ripshaw, also known as the Plague Doctor, made his way around to the driver's side of the truck, Watson reached into his pocket and pulled out the note Carmen gave him as he read it to himself.

"I told you this note would give you his location. What you do next is up to you. Do you want to be associated with La Lechuza? Earn it, maybe the next time I see you, I may tie you up."

Watson folded the note and placed it in his pocket. He then proceeded into the truck.

Chapter 6

Laney recovered relatively well from her horrible night out. Though her dreams from the last two nights had featured images of the red-eyed creature she had encountered just days earlier. Specifically, its body. The muscles in this creature's thighs bulged; they looked firm, and the greyish skin wrapped tightly around those muscles made a lasting impression. Of course, she also kept thinking about its seductively impressive cock. The fact that Laney was so intrigued by the double-headed penis was all she seemed to think about. After all, she would rather the memory of the creature's junk than of her date's.

Laney got home from her afternoon classes at the college. She was getting dressed to go to work. She was able to get a job at the local hamburger drive-in, Chance's Burgers. She liked her job most of the time. She worked behind the counter making milkshakes. Laney's aunt would give her a ride after school.

Sometimes, her friend Jordie would pick her up as well, since Jordie was a waitress at the restaurant. Jordie was the closest thing Laney had to a friend. She never judged Laney for being smart or for her weight, as others had at school. One thing Jordie admired about Laney was her toughness. She stayed to herself, primarily knowing that Laney wouldn't just put up with people's crap.

A car pulled up outside Laney's house, a white Chevy Corvette; the driver honked the horn.

Laney grabbed her purse as she walked out the door to meet Jordie, walked over to the vehicle, and hopped into the tight space of the car.

"Thanks for the ride."

"Of course, haven't heard from you in a couple of days, so I was getting worried. I figured you would never miss a work shift, so you would be ready for me to give you a lift."

"You know me, Ms. Reliable." Laney sighed and looked out of the passenger window. Jordie knew something was going on with Laney.

"You want to talk about anything? You seem a bit down."

Laney didn't want to tell her about the date she had with mister small dick and subsequently the encounter she had with mister rare dick. Also, it didn't help that a known fact around the college was that Jordie always had a thing for Brian, ever since high school.

Laney wanted to get things off her chest, metaphorically anyway.

"Okay, something has been bugging me, so I'll tell you, but keep it between us."

Jordie kept driving and nodded.

"Um, I had a date the other night. It didn't go well."

Jordie glanced over at Laney.

"Did some dirtbag try something with you? You tell me who it was, I'll knee them in the groin."

"No, Jordie. Nothing like that, he was just a jerk. Anyway, I think I am into an opposite type of being than what I dated."

Jordie gave out a loud cackle laugh that echoed in the small car chamber.

"Who was it?"

"Who was what?"

"Who was it you went on a date with? Someone from school?"

Jordie was inquisitive, and Laney felt that this could be one of those conversations that spiraled in a negative direction.

"You don't know him, some guy who showed up at work. Doesn't go to our school."

Jordie didn't buy it, but she didn't press the issue either and left it at that.

Laney couldn't stop thinking about that giant moth figure, the way he made Brian look like a scared little boy. The command he took of everything around him turned her on. She realized, once she was home later that night, that she had been in a state of panic and arousal at the sight of the beast. Something she swore to herself, she would never admit out loud.

Laney and Jordie finished their shifts at different times that night, so Laney's aunt picked her up from work and took her home.

Laney went into her room and changed into her red nightie.

She slid into bed, took off her round glasses, and stared at the ceiling, tired from a day of work and school, but the creature that looked like a moth stayed on her mind.

Laney closed her eyes and relived the scene that unfolded that night.

In her mind, it was as if Brian wasn't even there. Seeing the creature excited her. She reached her hand down under her slip, moving aside her panties, she began to gently stroke and play with her pubic hair, twirling it, passing her finger through the top, imagining she was touching the skin of the creature with the red eyes. Her hand then passed down to her clit, spreading her pussy lips apart ever so gently. She slowly rotated in a circular motion and began biting her bottom lip.

The thought of the creature's forked tongue sliding up and down under her clit made her spread two fingers down and up to simulate the motion of the tongue sliding its way between her labia, caressing those lips in a gentle but firm way. She moved her left hand down over the top of her red slip and pinched her dark cherry nipple.

Laney was as turned on as she had ever remembered. She masturbated to take care of her needs, often thinking of a romantic rendezvous with some guy in school or some grown man who would come to the carhop frequently. This felt different to her, almost a primal urge. She let out a soft moan, just low enough for her aunt downstairs not to be able to hear her.

She took two of her fingers and glided them in and out of her, as the palm of her thumb would rub her clit with every in and out motion. She thought of being naked in front of the creature, begging for the giant moth to tell her what to do.

She pinched her nipple harder, imagining the creature placing his strong claw hands on her throat and squeezing just tight enough to let her know he was her master and in control.

The thought ravaged her mind and body. She stopped squeezing her nipple and moved her hand around her throat, practically clawing at her neck as she pleasured herself.

Her feet began to slightly push up off the bed, jolting her body slightly. Her pussy was gushing wet, the drips were coming out of her and sliding around her fingers, down her taint onto the back of her panties, and onto the white bed sheet under her body.

Laney slid her fingers out of her. She went back to working her clit in a slow circular motion, and right as she was envisioning reaching for the creature's two-headed cock, she climaxed hard. She moved her hand from around her neck and covered her mouth to contain her pleasured scream. Her body shivered slightly as her toes curled and gripped the bed sheets. With one final burst, her body relaxed. Laney was in a euphoric malaise.

She was panting, trying to catch her breath. Before she slipped off into sleep, she couldn't help but wonder out loud.

"What the fuck is wrong with me?"

Chapter 7

Watson was halfway to his destination. The car that belonged to Ripshaw was humming down the road. Watson must kill Ripshaw, but he has no idea how or when to do it. The ride had been a mostly quiet one. Watson was lost in his thoughts; Ripshaw was not much of a talker. That combination made for an eerily silent drive until Watson spoke.

"Ripshaw, that is an interesting name. What is the origin of your name?"

Ripshaw huffed and kept driving, shifting himself slightly in the driver's seat.

"Ripshaw is just a nickname. Don't really mean much, I suppose."

Watson seemed to be better equipped at pulling teeth than having a conversation with the man whose life he was going to end. Still, Watson gave it another valiant effort. He was hoping that if he could see a glimmer of who this man was, perhaps he could make the argument to Carmen to spare the Plague Doctor's life.

"So, what can I expect from the town of Twain? Anything interesting to do there?"

"No, not really, it's a whisper of a town. What brings you here?"

"I am here to see my friend Mr. Sherlock Holmes."

"Well, I figured that much from your accent and clothes. I gave him a lift into town as well."

Watson stayed silent momentarily, thinking of what to say next.

"If you could please take me to Bedford Farm, Sherlock has accommodations there."

"Sure can, but I thought I was taking you to the Green-Eyed Motel?"

"I will find my way there. I must see my partner. It has been far too long; we have much to discuss."

"No problem, I know the way."

"So, Mr. Ripshaw, is this what you do for a living? Transport people from train stations and airports?"

Watson needed to break through that guarded demeanor the Plague Doctor was utilizing as part of his silent charm.

"No, sir, I am a doctor."

Ripshaw clarified.

"Don't worry, I'm not that kind of doctor."

"Then what kind of doctor are you. I have a doctorate in Medicine. Are you also a medical physician?

"Negative, Doctor."

Ripshaw did not answer the question; he kept driving down the vast stretch of highway, surrounded by mountains, well past the city. Watson attempted a different tactic to get Ripshaw to talk.

"Well, if you ever feel sick, I will be more than happy to help you while I am in town. Couldn't help but notice you have a cough."

The Plague Doctor reacted; it was quick and just a moment, but Watson caught the physical sign of distress. The chink in the armor, Ripshaw gripped the steering wheel harder, making a noise as his palm rubbed the plastic wheel.

Watson knew that a slight reaction to his health meant Ripshaw was bothered by the topic, or maybe that was just what Watson was trying to convince himself of.

"No need to worry about me, Doctor Watson, I'm doing just fine."

"If you say so." Watson left that comment floating in the middle of the air like a piece of bait waiting to catch a fish."

"What kind of medicine did you say you practice, again, Doctor Watson?"

"I asked you first."

Watson turned to Ripshaw and smiled, happy with his snarky reply. Nonetheless, Ripshaw answered him.

"I am a doctor of chemistry; I guess you could say."

"Ahh, chemistry, now that is a topic that has always interested me quite a bit. Only took a few courses while achieving my doctorate in medicine."

Watson let out a loud sigh.

"Please slow down, I am feeling a bit car sick, I may need to vomit."

Ripshaw pulled over to the side of the mountainous highway.

Watson looked at the Plague Doctor.

"I guess you can say I am a trauma doctor."

With his left elbow, Watson slammed it into the nose of Ripshaw. As the blood began gushing, Ripshaw, still recovering from the shock, Watson grabbed the back of Ripshaw's head and slammed it into the steering wheel, creating a loud thud.

Dazed and woozy, Watson slammed the driver's head again into the steering wheel, causing Ripshaw to pass out and slump over Watson. Watson patted the Plague Doctor's shoulder.

"If I am to kill you, I will need some information first."

Watson slid out of the passenger side of the truck, causing Ripshaw to fall onto the passenger seat. Watson went around the driver's side, got into the car, put it in drive, and continued onto the highway.

Chapter 8

The woods hold secrets tighter than a nun's ass. What the woods see, oftentimes, no one else does. Indeed, the forest could be a creepy place, but not if you are an experienced hiker like Rumley Whitaker. Born and raised in West Virginia, he loved the woods at any time of day. Though dark and dense, Rumley was navigating his way through the leafy pillars of earth as he would often do. He found a decent spot to camp for the night, figured he would get some shut-eye under the stars, and wake up to continue his journey. Things hardly ever turn out the way we think they will, at least not the way we play them out in our heads.

As he settled down for the evening, Rumley started a small campfire. He always carried a lighter and a piece of tinder on his hikes. Within seconds, he had a decent fire going; within minutes, it was enough flame and heat to at least keep one person warm.

He took a long, deep breath, feeling the flames giving off wisps of heat on his face. Then, out of the corner of his eye, he saw two red glowing lights. As his eyes adjusted and zoomed out, those eyes were attached to something significant, something lurking in the shadows.

A winged figure emerged, the likes of which Rumley had never seen in the woods or in civilization—the figure then expanded its wings in one loud flutter.

****

"Easy now, weakling, this will be your last trip in the woods, especially in that ridiculous outfit."

Rumley grabbed a branch from the top of the campfire flame and threw it towards the Mothman.

"You fucking shit, you almost burned me."

The Mothman's eyes burned in rage. Rumley was struggling to get to his feet, but it made no difference.

"Let's see how you enjoy this ride as you run away."

The winged beast flew over Rumley and lowered his talons to pick him up by his shoulders. His talons pierced each shoulder to ensure he had a good grip on him.

Rumley screamed in agony.

"Leave me alone, you fucking monster!"

"So, a monster is what I am, am I? Let me show you a true monster. Let's drop your body right onto this fire you made. There you go, enjoy that fire burning your back as you scramble to escape."

Rumley scampering away from the fire while pieces of char and smoke were coming off his khaki button-down short-sleeve shirt.

The Mothman expanded his wings into the night sky and flew down, landing on Rumley. He grabbed his neck and cracked it to one side like an egg. As the blood began gushing out, the Mothman began drinking the hiker's blood like a water fountain that wouldn't stop running.

Once Mothman got his fill, he grabbed Rumley's body and tossed it into the fire, flying away into the forest night to leave the woods with yet another secret.

Chapter 9

Watson wasn't exactly sure what his next move was. He followed the sign off the highway that led in the direction of the town of Twain. The Plague Doctor slumped in the truck's bench seat on the passenger side. Watson panicked when he attacked Ripshaw. He made a mistake without knowing what his next move would be. For a man as calculated as Watson, this was a massive error of judgment.

Surely, a town as small as Sherlock described would recognize a stranger driving a local's truck. Watson needed a plan, and quickly; unfortunately, he did not have one. Nor did he know how to communicate with Carmen.

The thought of Carmen sparked an idea for Watson. If he could find the local library, the one where Carmen's daughter works, she would help him. After all, killing the Plague Doctor was Carmen's idea.

Watson drove into the town of Twain, a small city with brick buildings arranged in parallel rows on opposite sides of the street. It was the kind of small country town he read about. Sherlock described the place very accurately.

He slowed the truck as it passed the storefronts, ensuring he was going just fast enough so that no one could see his comatose passenger next to him.

Then, out of the corner of his eye, he saw the small sign hanging down over an awning that read "*Library*".

Watson pulled the truck up to the side of the library and parked. He glanced over at the half-alive person next to him.

"Stay there."

After there was no movement from Ripshaw, Watson was satisfied he wouldn't move.

"Good."

The British doctor climbed out of the truck, closed the door, and walked into the library in the town of Twain.

As he walked into the library, he took a quick stock of who was there. There was no one, and Watson typically hasn't had great experiences in empty libraries. Then, a woman with red-rimmed glasses emerged.

"Dr. Watson, I presume. I am Carmina. What on earth are you doing in my domain?"

Watson hesitated; there was a slight resemblance to Carmen.

"Your mother gave me a task, and things didn't go as planned. I may need some assistance."

Carmina skeptically raised an eyebrow. She knew Watson landed in Atlanta earlier in the day. There was no way he needed help already.

"You just landed in Georgia; there is no way you could already be in over your head."

Watson was frustrated; he felt he needed to explain himself, but time was not on his side.

"If you would be so kind as to accompany me outside?"

Carmina followed Watson; they both approached the vehicle. She peered into the passenger side window and saw a slumped Ripshaw.

Carmina looked at Watson, and he returned a nervous smile.

"So, you did not follow my mother's instructions? Yes, I know what you were supposed to do, she told me. She also told me you were supposed to visit Sherlock first. How could you have fucked things up at such a miraculous speed?"

Watson did not need the lecture; he just needed help figuring out what to do next. Asking Sherlock was not an option.

"I am aware of my assignment. I wanted to get some answers from him before I…" He did not finish his sentence, but he didn't need to. Carmina knew what he meant.

"Fine, for La Lechuza, I have to help you."

"Around back there is a bicycle. You will take the road on the opposite side of the post office. It is paved but will eventually turn into a dirt road. Once you arrive at the dirt road, hide the bicycle in the trees. You will then walk the rest of the way to the Bedford farm. It will be a mile down the dirt road, and you will see moss covering a white picket fence. That is the Beford Farm."

Watson processed the information the moment Carmina said it, which led him to the very terrifying conclusion that she had done this sort of thing quite a few times before.

"Do you understand?"

Watson nodded.

"Good, tonight you will stay with Sherlock. Tomorrow I will pick you up and take you to your motel."

They both stood there as Carmina grew irritated at Watson's lack of movement.

"What the fuck are you waiting for? Get the bicycle and leave before anyone in town sees you!"

Watson began walking quickly towards the back of the building and found the bicycle. It was a mode of transportation Carmina always kept handy in case she had to travel more discreetly.

Watson climbed onto the bike and began to pedal.

****

Sherlock was getting Thor and himself ready for their nightly ritual, making some hot tea, and snuggling by the fire.

An unexpected knock came at Sherlock's shack door. It was an odd occurrence, since the only one who would knock was Myra, the owner of the farm, who Sherlock knew spent most of her nights fucking in the woods.

Sherlock walked over to the door and was surprised to see a sweaty and tired-looking Watson standing at the door.

"Watson?!"

"What on earth are you doing here?"

Watson smiled at Sherlock.

"Good to see you as well, partner. May I come in?"

Sherlock moved aside so Watson could enter the humble cabin that looked an awful lot like a shack

Thor stared at Watson, very unimpressed at the surprise appearance, walked around in a circle, and plopped himself down to begin his slumber.

"Thor, always a pleasure," Watson stated sarcastically, and luckily, living with Sherlock, Thor was used to sarcasm.

"Watson, is everything alright? Why are you here?"

"Not happy to see me, Sherlock?"

"Of course I am, you old fool, but I didn't know you were coming."

"I assume by the sweat on your brow and the blood on the elbow of your tweed jacket, you had quite the journey."

Damn it, Watson hated how observant Sherlock was. Now came the time for a story, one that he needed to spin enough for Sherlock to believe him.

"Well, I was working on a case. Jewel thief from Old Amersham. He left for the States, but I was hot on his trail. Evidence tells me he came through Twain, Georgia, on his way elsewhere. So here I am."

Sherlock wasn't buying the story.

"Did you have a run-in with the suspect?"

"Yes, we had a struggle, and well, he escaped. I need a place to rest for the night. I will continue the chase in the morning. The jewelry store offered our firm a handsome reward for his arrest."

Sherlock listened intently and then grabbed his cannabis cigarette from his nightstand and lit it.

A loud noise erupted from the nearby woods. It was a guttural, beastly sound. It was a sound Watson had never heard, followed by the pleasuring screams of a woman.

"Sherlock, what the hell was that?"

"Relax, Watson, that's just Skookum and Myra."

Sherlock could tell his partner looked confused.

"Sherlock, what the hell is a Skookum?"

"Oh, right, my apologies. Skookum is his proper name; I call him Bigfoot."

Still confused, Watson listened intently to the sounds. The moans of a woman being pleasured, the rustle of branches, a beast that sounded as if its bellows could make the very woods fearful of it.

"What the hell is a Bigfoot?"

"Elementary, my dear Watson."

"Don't be a fucking asshole, Sherlock, it isn't elementary. What the hell is that thing?"

"I am sorry, it seems we both have a lot of explaining to do. Let's have some tea and get some rest. In the morning, I will tell you about the experience that brought me here, in more detail than we previously discussed."

Watson nodded in agreement. He was exhausted and couldn't help but think that he still had a man somewhere in town that he needed to kill.

Chapter 10

Laney could not stop thinking about the creature she had seen, which looked like a giant moth. While sitting in her sociology class, it was all she could think about. Earlier in the day, Brian saw her from across the courtyard and turned to continue walking with his friends. The bruised nose that adorned his face brought a smile to her face.

However, now she found herself thinking about the creature. She was always a fan of the occult, the unexplained, and apparently, now she was also into the perverse monster.

She couldn't explain it, but ever since she looked into the creature's eyes, she felt connected to it as if the pines and woods of West Virginia were beckoning her to go back to where she saw him.

What if it killed her?

What if this creature wanted to tear her apart?

It was a risk she weighed, but she also knew what it was like when the creature looked at her body and took her in. The creature's cock came out in full display, and she likes to think somewhere in her brain that she deserves the credit for that. The thought made her joyful and confident.

She needed to get back to the woods. Now she had to figure out how to do that. She couldn't go with anyone else; they would freak out. What if they got hurt? That would dig deep into her conscience for the rest of her life.

No, this was something Laney wanted to do; she had to do it alone.

As she drowned out the professor's lecture, thinking about seeing the creature again, she developed a plan. A plan that required some lying, a small amount of theft, which she convinced herself was an act of borrowing, and a shit ton of courage.

Laney's plan wasn't overly complicated. She would go to work, ask her only friend to borrow her car to check in on her aunt, who she would claim was sick. She would return before her work shift was over. It would give her four whole hours to make it to the woods, explore the creature, and return to work.

That was the plan. Laney was going to see it through.

Chapter 11

Laney was getting ready for work; she didn't like how her pale-yellow uniform skirt fit her, but it was part of the job. She felt it made her look like a stuffed banana. She packed some clothes to change into once she escaped from her night shift. Looking through her closet, she did not know what clothes to change into. Black was her preferred absence-of-color clothing, something that often made her stand out in a world of pastels. She lived in a world of rock 'n' roll, but the fast-paced, hopping sounds did not match her personality. For that reason, Laney was an avid lover of classical music; she felt it had a haunting tone that resonated with her.

She chose a pleated dress. Though it was tight on her curves, she felt the black tone would help her blend into the woods. She tightly packed it into her handbag.

Unsure why exactly she was concerned about how she looked for this expedition. Maybe it was to please the monster, or perhaps to please herself.

Jordie's car horn sounded. Laney packed the last of her items and made her way down the stairs.

"Bye, Tia."

"Bye, Laney, have a good day at work."

With the closing of the front door, Laney was fast approaching her friend's vehicle.

Once inside, Laney had to lay the groundwork to be able to borrow Jordie's car later.

"Hey, my friend, what's with the make-up? You have a hot date after work?"

Laney gave a nervous laugh and shrugged.

Jordie began driving away from Laney's house.

"Are you feeling better, Laney?"

Of course she was, she pleasured herself to the visions of the monster and climaxed so hard, her entire body shivered.

"I'm fine, Jordie. I am just a bit worried about my Tia."

Jordie, being Laney's friend, was slowly picking up Spanish; along with a few courses she took in high school, this helped her understand certain words.

"Is something wrong with your aunt?"

This was phase one of Laney's plan. For the record, phase two was getting the vehicle from Jordie, and phase three was driving to the woods. Laney thought it best not to add any further phases to her plan, as she knew it all hinged on the first three going off without a hitch.

"Yeah, she hasn't been feeling well. Since it's just the two of us, I offered to stay home and take care of her, but she is too proud to let me play nurse."

"That sucks. I hope she feels better."

"Once we are at work, I'll give her a call to check up on her. You know me, I'm a worrywart."

Jordie, being the understanding friend, nodded; she never took her eyes off the road.

"I totally get it. If it were my mom or aunt, I would be worried as well."

They sat in mostly silence until they got to Chance's Burgers. Luckily, it seemed busy. This boded well for Laney; the busier the restaurant was, the less likely it was that someone would notice her missing for an extended period during her shift.

They began their shift. Laney intently kept looking up at the round clock as the second hand slowly turned. Thirty minutes in, enough time for her to pretend to call her aunt and check in on her.

Laney noticed how busy Jordie was—running orders back and forth from different cars. This was her chance. When Jordie approached the counter, Laney presented her story.

"Jordie, I just called my aunt, and she didn't answer. Maybe she just fell asleep, but I am worried about her. Could you cover me while I check on her? If I can borrow your car, I won't be long, promise."

Jordie was in one of those moments where she was juggling various tasks. She trusted Laney. So, she agreed to lend Laney her car, only with slight hesitation.

"Just be quick; if old man Chance catches you on the clock skipping work, he will fire you on the spot."

Bubba Chance, the sixty-year-old local who treated his workers like crap and always had a wandering eye for the younger women working in his burger joint. He had the personality of warm cat piss, but Laney needed the money, so she tolerated him as best she could.

Laney knew how to drive. She had her driver's license and sometimes drove her aunt on errands around town.

Laney knew the route down State Route 62. The pine trees on both sides lined the road. There were plenty of areas to drive into the woods, though not paved. She felt a pull drawing her where to go. She couldn't describe it exactly, but it felt like a giant magnet in her chest, aching to be closer to something.

The car slowed down. Laney turned onto a road that could have been the same one Brian took her through on their disastrous date, though she couldn't be sure.

She pulled in just enough until there were only woods surrounding her. The eager Laney took the opportunity to change out of her work outfit and put on the black dress she brought. Trying to get her uniform off wasn't difficult; she tossed it onto the passenger seat, along with the weight of a job she did not like.

However, putting on the black dress was not as easy.

"This fucking car was made for twigs. How the hell is a plump girl supposed to change in this tuna can?"

She was talking to herself, of course, a characteristic that seemed to appear more often.

Laney exited the vehicle and left the door open. She glanced around. There wasn't a living soul in proximity to her. This was her perfect opportunity to put on the black dress she brought with her quickly.

She grabbed the dress from her handbag, feeling exposed, wearing only her black bra and matching black lace panties.

As Laney began to slip on her dress, she heard a noise from above her. She looked up in a panic, not knowing what to expect, but she saw nothing. She knew the moth creature was close by; she could feel him near her. That magnetism she felt in her chest was getting closer, tighter.

Which could only mean that what she came looking for would soon be present.

However, no moth creature appeared. Wanting to take control of the situation and not wanting to feel helpless, she shouted at the night sky.

"Where are you?!"

"Come out so I can see you!"

Her request went unanswered, so Laney leaned into the car and pushed hard on the horn. She abandoned the idea of putting her dress on, after all, the monster had already seen her breasts.

The car horn's noise did nothing to bring the Mothman out.

In one final attempt to get his attention, Laney had a brilliant yet dangerous idea. Laney unclasped her bra and tossed it in front of Jordie's car. The headlights shone on the bra a few paces away from the hood.

Laney remembered how intently the Mothman was staring at her round and heavy hanging tits.

Her idea worked. From the shadows, Mothman emerged on the opposite side of the bra.

She wasn't exactly sure what to do next. The Mothman took a step closer. She could see his bright red eyes emerging from the darkness. Those red eyes stared at her intently. Laney moved one step closer as they stared at each other.

"What, what are you?" Her voice trembled with fear and exhilaration, the kind of emotional blend that makes your heart race.

Then something happened that caught her completely off guard. The beastly winged creature spoke back.

"I am many things."

His voice had a raspy, husky edge.

"You can speak? How?"

"This form you see me in isn't always how I have traversed this world."

The plumped, filled body of Laney entranced Mothman, his eyes fixated on her form.

"My name is Laney; I was here a few nights ago…"

The Mothman stopped her from explaining further.

"I know, I remember you... all of you."

"Do you have a name?"

Her curiosity ran wild, and she wanted to know as much as possible about this creature.

"I am the Mothman... but you can call me Vlad."

"Do you live in the woods?"

Mothman stepped closer to Laney, but she did not take a step back. The more she communicated with the creature, the more comfortable she felt.

"I live in this forest; it is all my home."

Mothman watched Laney's breath as her chest filled in and out with air.

"When you chased the car the other night, you looked at me, I felt something I do not know how to describe, but I haven't been able to stop thinking about what you are and why you are here."

He stepped closer, and so did Laney. Now they were only a few feet apart.

"When I looked at you, I imprinted a part of me on you. It draws you closer to me, you can feel where I am and how to find me."

"Why would you do that?" Her voice cracked just a little as the words flowed out of her mouth.

He did not answer, but he got closer to her, now just a foot apart. She looked up at him, his leather skin, the feathers that adorned parts of his body.

"Why do you keep looking at me like that?" Laney was getting frustrated, wanting more answers than Vlad was willing to provide.

"I have not seen such beauty in my lifetime. I wanted to make sure I could see you again."

The compliment took Laney back. Turns out the nicest thing a male has ever said to her came from a creature that would make the average man shit his pants.

"You think I am beautiful? Seriously?"

Mothman put his arms and claw-like hands around her lower back and pulled her close. She instantly felt that powerful magnetism to be complete. There was no longer her chest pulling closer to him because she was already there, in its arms.

Unsure of what to do, she placed her hand on his feathery chest, giving her the option to push away the moment she felt uncomfortable. But she didn't feel uncomfortable; she felt whole.

"You know the other night, I was in bed... thinking of you."

"What did you do, Laney, when you were in bed thinking of me?"

"Show me."

Vlad said, his glowing eyes staring down at her.

Laney pushed Mothman slowly backwards. He took two steps back; she walked over to the open car door and sat down, facing Mothman. She leaned back on the seat, and with her right hand, she grabbed her right breast. She began slowly squeezing her nipple and slightly tugging on it.

Her left hand moved down and pushed aside her black panties, showing Vlad her delicate flower. As she began to rub her pussy lips gently, Vlad's eyes grew brighter red. He stared intently, wanting to devour her at that moment.

Laney wanted to be in control; she liked the struggle of giving demands and taking them. As her eyes faced the beige ceiling of the car, she felt a tongue touching her fingers.

She moved her fingers to spread her pussy lips, but it wasn't necessary.

Mothman's forked tongue licked her and spread her pussy lips open with his strong tongue. No one had ever eaten her before. She moved her hand and grabbed his clawed digits. Vlad brought his claw-like hand up and wrapped it around her throat, just as she imagined in her bedroom. Did she will this beastly encounter? Or did they enjoy the same pleasures as their bodies were connected?

As the Mothman continued to pass his forked tongue up her pussy, her clit splitting the tongue as it caressed both sides of her.

"Squeeze my throat harder." She begged as she moaned in pleasure. He obeyed her command.

Laney looked down to see that he was on his knees outside the car. She couldn't move her head down too much because of the restraint he had on her throat.

Mothman licked her down to her taint and then slithered his tongue into her. She cried out in ecstasy. His wings expanded and popped out in full bloom as he continued devouring her with his tongue.

One of his finger talons from around her neck crept its way into her mouth, and she began suckling on it; it was instinctual. Everything she experienced and did felt right for her. She wasn't ashamed of her weight, of her obscure style; she was enjoying a massive creature pleasuring her.

Vlad, while still having his tongue in her, softly nibbled on her pussy.

"Do it again." She clamored in between breaths. Mothman must have been caught up enjoying her flesh, because he continued but did not bite.

"I said, do it again!" The command in her voice felt strong, powerful, and fearless. Vlad obliged and bit her pussy again.

He removed his tongue from her and began slapping it up and down slowly as if he were painting her with his tongue.

****

"She tastes so good. Her softness on my tongue, her black hair surrounding her pussy, tickles me as I pleasure her in and out with it. Her body is amazing. She is lying on her back, seeing her meaty stomach, it beckons me."

Mothman continued his oral gratification of Laney, making her more comfortable. She placed her ankles on his shoulders, and he didn't mind that it was hitting his wings with every thrust of his tongue as her body slowly moved up and down.

"Eat my pussy, you fucking monster!"

Monster... Vlad hated that term, but not when Laney said it. For him, her command was a turn-on; it heightened his desire for her. She used his shoulder to kick off her shoe from the back of the heel.

"She is squeezing my hand around her throat harder. Let me oblige."

Laney loved it; the harder he squeezed, the more she moaned.

His tongue continued to caress her soft flower, lapping up all the moistness her body had to offer. Then she began breathing heavier, moaning louder.

"She is enjoying this, so am I. Let me try pulling my tongue slowly out and back in a few times."

"There we go, now she is shaking slightly, she is about to erupt, I feel it. The way her pussy lips are gripping my tongue, the way my hand is feeling the pulse from her throat."

As Laney began to climax, her pussy began to squirt. First, a few drops, then a good amount more, shooting out of her right into Mothman's mouth.

"That is new, caught a little on my face, but it tastes so good, a sweet nectar that only this gorgeous creature can create."

Laney's legs went weak as her body began to shiver. She closed her eyes tightly as her body went through a few more shakes, and then pure relaxation took over her soul. Her chest felt lighter, her head in a heavenly state.

"Good, now remove your hand from my throat."

"I will listen to her this time, but before I do, I am going to pass my hand slowly over her breasts so I can feel her nipples."

Laney smiled as the creature did this.

Mothman, however, kept licking her. Her clit was sensitive, and she needed a moment to recoup from the last orgasm.

"Stop it, Vlad. I need a moment."

Mothman ignored her and continued to lick her clit up and down.

"I said stop!" Laney used her exposed foot to hit him on the head lightly.

Mothman stopped and took a few crawling paces back away from the car.

Laney sat up in the car, still sitting on the driver's side seat, staring at Vlad.

"When I say stop, you stop; when I say harder, I mean harder."

She shocked herself; it didn't sound like her words that were coming out of her mouth, but they were her words, every syllable of them.

"You wish to command me?"

The now satisfied Laney snapped to the reality that she was talking to a creature, a strong, sexy monster.

"Yes, I do." She replied confidently.

She was honest when she said yes; she knew, when they melted into each other in the car, that he listened to her and would do what she said.

Mothman felt something he hadn't felt before in his existence as a creature of the night, whether a giant moth or a vampire. He felt owned.

"She wishes to be my master. I will allow this sexy woman to do just that."

"Yes, master."

"Master? Me?"

Even Laney thought this might have gone too far, but she loved the idea of telling someone or something to do what she wanted to her and having it done.

Mothman nodded. Laney beckoned him with her finger, and he began to move towards her until she told him to stop.

"Stop!"

Vlad obeyed and stopped, though he was confused because she had called him with her finger.

"Crawl to me."

Her voice was edgy and stern.

"She wants me to crawl. I will crawl for her and drag my body to her feet."

"Very good." Laney smiled at him, content that he was following directions.

She leaned down and grabbed the side of his face with her hands. She kissed him on his gray lips.

Staring at him intently, she asked him what she truly wanted to know.

"Would you really do anything for me?"

Mothman's eyes burned a dark red; the vibrant glow now went dull as he looked into her brown eyes.

"My darling, I will burn the world down for you."

Vlad said in a powerful tone.

"Then we will bathe in the heat of the world burning."

Her reply made him rest his head on her voluptuous breasts.

Chapter 12

Watson and Sherlock awoke the next morning.   Sherlock told Watson briefly about the Bigfoot case that brought him to North America.

Much of Sherlock's story was hard to believe. Though Watson knew it wasn't more difficult to accept than a secret society of witches and monsters that he now happens to be associated with. Watson made no mention of his actual reason for being in Twain, Georgia.

Sherlock explained that the mysterious stories from around the states had intrigued him, and he would stay until he found his next big case.

"So, Sherlock, you are telling me, somewhere in that forest is the beast that Ms. Myra Bedford asked you to investigate?"

Watson pointed out of the small shack window.

"That is correct."

"Myra Bedford fell in love with the beast, and they have sex in the woods almost regularly."

Watson remarked incredulously.

"Two for two, dear Watson."

"And you saw this beast with your own two eyes?"

"Indeed, I did, quite the sight actually."

Sherlock had gotten used to the events that had happened a few months ago when he arrived.

"So, Sherlock, if you believe this Skookum, Bigfoot, whatever you call it, killed the sheriff, why didn't you do something? Why didn't you tell the authorities?"

"Not that simple, dear friend. The sheriff was a corrupt man. He also felt that he would take liberties of a sexual nature with Ms. Bedford. Skookum was defending her."

Watson allowed that last statement to sink in for a moment.

"Is there anything else?"

Sherlock felt best not to mention that Bigfoot killed Myra's abusive husband. The information he provided Watson with was enough for one day.

"No, my friend, that is the gist of what transpired."

"What's your next case going to be? Dragons?"

Sherlock appreciated Watson's sarcastic tone.

There was a knock on the door. Sherlock answered, it was Carmina. Watson instantly became nervous. Forgetting for a moment, he attacked another man, and Carmina was helping him clean up his mess.

"Carmina, what a great surprise to see you this morning."

Sherlock liked Carmina more than just as a friend.

"Good morning, Sherlock. I came right over because I received this article from Point Pleasant, West Virginia. I think this may be the case you have been waiting for."

Carmina handed over the article to Sherlock and peered over his shoulder to find a confused Watson sitting there.

"Who's your friend, Sherlock?"

Watson was not surprised at how well she could lie. It was a skill that seemed to be second nature to her.

"How terribly rude of me, this is my partner from London, Dr. John Watson."

"Very pleased to meet you, Mr. Watson."

"Doctor Watson."

He corrected her flatly. Sherlock was not much for titles; he ignored the contempt in Watson's voice.

"A mistake I surely will not make again. My apologies."

Carmina shot Watson an innocent smile that made his stomach turn. He knew that under that perfect grin was the daughter of a witch—a witch who happened to control a powerful secret society and his fate.

Sherlock began looking over the article Carmina brought him as he read it aloud.

"Another missing person in the woods of Point Pleasant, West Virginia. Yet another person who claimed they were going hiking or camping has gone missing. Locals are scared to go into the woods as they claim there may be a serial killer on the loose. Some locals have claimed to have seen a large, red-eyed flying creature in the night sky, moving at high speed. Teenagers have been warned not to visit the woods, as it has long been a popular spot for making out. Whatever is happening in the forest has local law enforcement baffled and residents scared."

Watson glanced at Carmina, who then glanced at Sherlock as he stared at the article.

"This is it! This is the case I have been waiting for. A supposed winged creature is terrorizing citizens in the forest. There must be something more to it."

"Sherlock, surely you can choose something a little less... cryptid-like."

Watson knew monsters were real; he had no choice but to believe that simple fact. Though he felt Sherlock was the best detective in the world, he believed chasing creatures of the night was not the best way to spend his time.

"Perhaps you should rethink this one, Sherlock…"

Before John Watson could continue, Carmina cut his verbal persuasion.

"Sherlock, that sounds fantastic. I know you have been searching for a while, so when I saw this case, I knew it would be a good fit for you. I've driven to West Virginia before. I will gladly drive you there if you pay for gas."

That is all it took for Sherlock to be convinced.

"It's settled, Thor, we are headed to Point Pleasant, West Virginia. Watson, dear friend, it was a pleasure seeing you, but it seems we both have cases to attend. You are welcome to stay here while I am gone."

"Oh, Sherlock, don't be silly. We have a motel in town. Watson can come and go as he pleases, and it would be easier for him to have the conveniences of the town closer to where he is staying."

Carmina was a fucking expert at persuasion and at managing situations. In one visit, she had Sherlock investigate the case she wanted, then had Watson stay at the location of her choice.

"I'm headed back to town and will gladly give Dr. Watson a ride back."

"Very well, Carmina, if you could just allow me one moment with my colleague, he will be on his way."

Sherlock and Carmina exchanged smiles.

"Of course, I will be waiting in the car."

Carmina exited the small shack and headed towards her vehicle.

Sherlock went to his bed and removed a revolver from under his pillow. He handed it to Watson.

"Look, Watson, we do not have much time. Whatever is going on, I know you have not told me the truth about why you are here. Take this revolver. I purchased two of them when I arrived in Georgia. Should you need it, do not hesitate to use it."

Watson glanced at Sherlock and nodded his head. He took the revolver and tucked it into the waistband of his wool pants. Sherlock gave him a coat to conceal his weapon.

"Sherlock, do you trust Carmina?"

"As much as anyone can trust someone they have known for a mere few months, Watson."

Watson took a step closer to Sherlock.

"She isn't who she says she is."

They stared at each other. The tension in the air was thicker than mountain fog on an early morning.

"Time to go, Watson."

They shook hands and patted each other's shoulders.

As Watson was headed out the door, Sherlock called out to him.

"Watson, once I arrive in West Virginia, I will send word that I arrived safely."

As Watson began walking towards the car, he heard Bigfoot moan in the woods again.

Watson turned back to Sherlock.

"They fuck all morning too?"

Sherlock shrugged as Watson shook his head and walked off the small porch.

Chapter 13

Laney woke up the next day feeling like a new woman. Her plan went perfectly, except for the part when she got tongue fucked by a monster and squirted in his mouth. That part was not planned at all, but she was glad it happened.

She made it back to Chance's Burgers before her shift was over. Bubba Chance kept giving her odd looks, like he knew she was gone but did not say anything to her.

During her morning routine, she decided not to attend her college courses that day. Instead, she would try to find her way back to the woods, back to the Mothman. That magnetic sensation from inside her chest that was present the day before had returned.

She put on her cotton robe and made her way downstairs for breakfast. Her aunt was sitting at the small dining room table listening intently to the morning news broadcast.

As Laney slowly walked down the steps, she stopped and overheard the news.

"The hiker said to have gone missing several days ago is nowhere to be found. Some dried blood marks were found in the woods, but due to the rain, law enforcement could not determine if it was human blood or that of an animal."

"Everyone is encouraged not to descend into the woods, especially at night, until whoever is responsible for these disappearances is found."

Laney finished walking down the stairs and into the kitchen to grab herself some coffee. As a college student, she lived on coffee.

"Good morning."

"Good morning, Tia."

"What were you listening to?"

"The news, another person has gone missing in the woods. This time it was a hiker. You don't go there to hang out, do you?"

She paused, careful not to share too much with her aunt.

"Nah, I never go that way. Maybe it's like some big crazy bear out there or something eating these people."

That was Laney's way of defending her creature, her slave.

"Better than a serial killer, I suppose."

Her aunt felt reassured by Laney's response.

However, she was slightly panicked inside. She did not want innocent people to go missing. She knew inside that Vlad was surely the culprit, and she needed to find out.

"Tia, can I borrow the car tonight to go to work?"

"Of course you can, but I thought Jordie was picking you up for work like she always does."

Laney had to think quickly; another lie was getting ready to rampage out of her mouth.

"Jordie and I got into an argument. Like, we are totally fine, but you know, I wanted to have some space to cool off."

The only part of that statement that was true was that Laney and Jordie were totally fine.

Sure, Jordie questioned Laney about the wet spot in the driver's seat, but Laney did not give her an answer.

"Of course, I understand."

Her aunt Monica stated with understanding.

With her transportation to see Mothman later today secured, Laney drank her coffee and made her way back upstairs to recover from her sexually draining encounter.

****

Watson was in the car with Carmina, driving back into town. The ride was mostly silent; he did not ask her how she disposed of Ripshaw.

"What did you do with him?"

Watson asked as if he were asking about the weather—a calm demeanor on the outside, worry, concern, and self-hate on the inside.

"Listen up, I am not going to clean up your mess again. Try not to fuck things up. My mom wants you to stay in town until you complete your task."

Watson thought it was over. He thought Carmina would dispose of the passed-out Plague Doctor, and that would be it.

"You mean, I still have to kill him?"

Carmina glanced at Watson, with a very annoyed look on her face, then looked back at the road she was driving on.

"You didn't come all this way to pass the buck to someone else."

"What if I decide not to kill him? Then what?"

Watson's voice was defiant, but he knew the consequences of not finishing his assignment.

"John, you will kill Ripshaw or the Plague Doctor or whatever else you want to call him. If you don't kill him, I will…Then I will dismember Sherlock in front of you. I won't even begin to tell you what my mother would do with what would be left of you."

Watson got the point; he nodded and waved his hand at her in a fleeting motion, a physical expression of not wanting to hear anymore.

She pulled up to the Green-Eyed Motel and parked her car.

"Get the fuck out."

No sense in arguing with her, he exited the vehicle, before he could close the passenger side door; she tossed the keys to his motel room through the car door opening, landing at Watson's feet.

He slammed the door shut. Carmina drove off in haste as Watson bent down to pick up his room key.

He smiled when he realized the orange room keychain had the number 22 etched on it.

"What a coincidence."

He made his way up the stairs to the second floor. It was the only motel in town, a pasty mint green color with white doors. The fence wrapped around the second floor overlooking the pool. Watson found his room and put the key into the slot, turning the handle to open the door. He entered the dark room, passing his hand on the wall next to the entry door in search of a light switch.

He was so ready to have a moment to breathe, to unwind, and to wrap his head around everything that had happened in the last twenty-four hours.

Once he found the switch and flicked it on, the door slammed closed behind him.

Sitting in a chair in front of Watson was Ripshaw. He had bled from his face and head, but he was still alive and moving around. He had a burlap sack over his head and was shaking it back and forth. The muffled sounds coming from under the face covering told Watson that his mouth was gagged.

Looking at the bed, there was a black mask. The mask had a long crow beak attached to a zorro-style mask. There was no mistaking this: it was the Plague Doctor's mask. The leather seemed polished; metal studs were affixed to both sides of the mask and the beak.

Under the mask was a note. Watson picked up the mask with one hand and the note with the other.

"Do what I have asked of you, and I will let you tie me up next.. Love, Carmen"

Watson stared at the man sitting in the chair and looked down at the plague doctor mask. He dropped the note and pulled the mask over his head. Watson, now wearing the mask, walked over to Ripshaw and pulled the sack off Ripshaw's head.

Chapter 14

Laney drove her aunt's car down the north side of town on Route 62. She was pretty sure she could find the exact spot where she had her sexual rendezvous with Vlad. That magnetism in her chest began to get stronger again, and she could feel the pull within her body as she was getting closer to him. The trees zoomed past the vehicle in a blur; night had already begun to fall, setting the scene for a highway that would soon be desolate from cars.

She turned off in the area she had before, leading through the dirt road, the trees and brush surrounding her car until no more highway could be seen or heard. She stepped out of the car and let the weight of the door close with a slight push from her hip.

After taking a few steps, she stood there in the silence of the woods. The pull in her chest grew stronger; she knew he was close.

"Where are you?"

She screamed into the trees, knowing he could hear her. Then the flapping sound got closer to her. Mothman landed in front of Laney. He stood up, wings sprawled, and then slowly retracted them towards his back.

Laney still couldn't get over this creature; its skin was toned to an unearthly gray. The feathers covering his groin looked elegant somehow. She couldn't get distracted by her sexual urges now; she wanted answers.

"What the fuck did you do? Have you been killing people in the woods?"

Deep inside, Laney knew the answer, but she needed to hear it from him. Somewhere in her heart, she had hoped a denial was coming, but it did not.

"Yes, I have."

Vlad's voice was rich; the grunting sound he made while devouring her slipped into her mind.

"Why? Why would you do that?!"

"I must feed Laney; I need blood as substance."

"No more killing, you got that? You said you would do anything I say. No More killing!"

Mothman stared at her with his red glowing eyes.

"I must feed, and I need blood or…"

Vlad stopped mid-sentence. He wasn't sure how to tell her the truth, that her juices gave him more substance and power than blood when he tasted her. She wasn't always around, though, and he had to make do by feeding on the blood of others.

Laney looked at him in confusion.

"Or what, Vlad? What aren't you telling me?"

"I can live without blood."

"Great problem solved, no more killing."

Laney seemed satisfied with this answer.

"But I need you, Laney. When your natural juices flowed into my mouth, it gave me the power I needed; it invigorated me as I had never felt before. I can go without blood if you can feed me the way you did the other night."

She was taken aback. This murderous, winged creature could live if he ate her pussy the way he did the other night. The thought of her legs on his shoulder as his forked tongue caressed around her clit gave her goosebumps.

She snapped out of her reminiscing momentarily.

"Fine, I will feed you. Just, no more killing, okay?"

Mothman nodded and looked down to see Laney with her hand on his torso.

Her touch immediately excited him.

Laney passed her hand down until it reached the grouping of feathers that covered his cock. Her touch aroused him; his cock with two heads parted the feathers and appeared in front of her.

She recalled his cock hanging outside the car that first terrifying night they met. She couldn't stop thinking about it since then.

The Mothman's cock was thick; it split into two penis heads like his forked tongue.

Laney reached down and was able to grab both cock heads, one in each hand. Mothman had one long, thick shaft and two heads that were far enough apart for her to hold one in each hand.

She became empowered, knowing that the Mothman now relied on her to survive.

"Do you like it when I grab your cock?"

She looked at him and asked teasingly.

"Yes, master Laney."

"What should your master do with this cock?"

Laney fully embraced her role as his master and got wet just by having this magnificent creature under her control.

"Whatever madam wishes."

Laney looked down at her hands as she tugged on his head in each hand. They felt smooth and thick. She looked up at him, commanding him on what to do next.

"Stay still."

Laney kneeled and opened her mouth to slide one of his cock heads into her mouth, while slowly rubbing the other one. The grunting sound from Vlad began, and his fangs drew out from his mouth as he moaned.

She rolled her tongue around his cock head while it was in her mouth. She moved back as Mothman's cock made a suction noise as it popped out into the night air from her mouth. Laney proceeded to put the other cock head in her mouth and began sucking. She placed her hands behind his long legs, and she could feel them tremble, letting her know she was doing a great job at making him weak.

Vlad's wings expanded in one large flap. He attempted to place a hand on Laney's head while she was sucking him.

"No, hands off, I didn't tell you to touch me, did I?"

She was in charge; there was nothing he could do but take her command.

"No master."

He removed his claw-like hand from her head as she commanded.

She moved her mouth away from him, causing a string of saliva to attach from her lips to his cock, Laney looked up at the towering figure with her eyes that read innocent and deadly at the same time.

"Good boy," she said in a condescending tone.

She was still unsure how Mothman had a cock that looked human, except for the color, size, and two cock heads.

Laney put her tongue out and took turns slapping the heads on her tongue one at a time.

Holding his shaft, she could feel it pulsating; the warmth of the veins throbbing in her hand made her squeeze down on him harder.

Her mouth moved away, and Laney tugged and jerked both cock heads. She loved every moment of this.

"You." She tugged on his cock.

"Will."

"Not."

"Kill."

"Again."

With every word, she jerked his two cock heads.

"Yes, master, he hissed."

His primal anger subdued as Laney made him melt, first into her mouth and then into her hands. She was in control, and there was nothing he could do but take it and show his pleasure.

****

"It isn't fair what she is doing. How can she control me this way?"

Mothman looked down, watching Laney's eyes fixated on his glowing red beams staring down at her.

"Look at her face, those plump cheeks and devilish look. She enjoys telling me what to do. I will do anything for her sweet nectar again."

Laney kept tugging and felt that Vlad was going to cum, she tasted a bit of his sweet liquid, just a few drops from one fell on her hand, she licked her finger where the drop was, then she continued jerking his cocks.

"I am going to unload on her, I can feel it coming from my loins."

Vlad came, both cock heads spurting out cum at a steady stream. The hot seed hit Laney's face, and she instinctively moved the cocks to one side so the rest of it wouldn't fall on her. Mothman's cum splashed on her; it was warm like hot wax.

She looked up at him in a bit of shock. She wiped her face with her hand and, while staring at him, licked her palm where his monster juice ended up.

"She is so beautiful. I can't tell if she wants to tear me apart or devour me. I hope both."

"You came on me! Did your master tell you that you could cum?"

"No master but I couldn't help it."

"That's a bad Mothman."

She stood up from the ground, dusting off the dirt from her knees. Now, her next move was to establish more dominance over him.

"Follow me."

Laney walked past Mothman as his cock began to retract back behind the black feathers of his groin. The truth was, Laney did not know where she was going; she didn't know the forest or the woods, and she was making up her confidence as she went along.

She walked fifty paces into the trees and stopped, pointing to one large pine tree.

"This is your corner. When you are bad, you go to your corner and stay there until master tells you to come out. Do you understand, Vlad?"

Mothman nodded. The truth was that the more she commanded him, the harder his cock would become. She could see his two heads coming back out from under the feathers."

"No, not now. Go to your corner and stay there. Master will be back later."

Vlad stalked his tall figure behind the pine tree and then flew up to one of the branches above.

Laney looked up and smiled.

"Good Boy."

Chapter 15

Sherlock had his suitcase neatly packed and was ready to travel to Point Pleasant, with Thor in tow. After some brief research, Carmina determined that the best option for Sherlock to travel was by car.

Carmina, being a helpful individual, offered to drive Sherlock the 12 hours it was estimated to take.

Also, it gave her an excuse to get out of town and leave Watson to fend for himself. This trip would ensure Sherlock was taken directly to where he needed to be to investigate the winged creature.

"Carmina, I cannot thank you enough for offering to drive me. I will compensate you for your time, I promise."

"No need to thank me, Sherlock; it is my pleasure. Plus, this is significantly cheaper than driving to Atlanta and flying from there."

Sherlock and Carmina entered the truck that was once Ripshaw's. Sherlock knew this truck; he had been in it before. After hearing Watson's warning about Carmina, he decided it was best not to mention that he knew the car was stolen.

"Not your usual ride, Carmina. Where is your car?"

"Oh, this is my uncle's truck. He loaned it to me for the road trip; he figured the truck bed could be helpful to us, and the height gives us more visibility on the road."

"Very fair points your uncle makes, Carmina."

Sherlock knew the truck belonged to Ripshaw, but he decided not to bring him up, as it did not seem very important at the time.

As they began the drive, Sherlock asked about the itinerary.

"When do we make our first stop?"

"Well, we must drive for a while. We can stop over at a small motel in Roanoke, Virginia, and rest there for the night."

Sherlock nodded; he was familiar with the history of Roanoke and the missing colony. His knowledge of that context gave him an unnatural sense of comfort.

"Carmina, you seem to be as fascinated by these cryptid creatures as I am. What is your draw to them?"

"Same as yours, I would think, Sherlock. There are things on this earth that cannot be easily explained, and those are the things that interest me."

"That is all?" Sherlock asked inquisitively.

"Is that not enough? I figured as a detective, you could appreciate the interest of the unexplained."

"I certainly do, Carmina. Is that why you have helped me research these cases around North America?"

"I know you were looking for a special case, Sherlock. I just wanted to be close enough to see one of these cryptids."

"Have you seen monsters before, Sherlock?"

The detective leaned back in the truck bench seat. He thought of the victims he had seen in London of the Ripper. Flashes of blood from the hell hounds, and Skookum, a beast so big it would make any grown man wet their pants.

"I've seen monsters," Sherlock said as his voice drifted off.

"I've seen bodies mutilated, men who ravaged cities, dictators who killed innocent people. I've seen monsters, alright, but most of the monsters I have dealt with didn't have wings or look like werewolves. No, dear Carmina, the monsters I have seen were all flesh and blood in human form."

Carmina stayed silent; it was the first time in her dealings with Sherlock that she realized he was not just some crime stopper. He was a man who saw things that no man should ever see, and that one realization made her respect him more.

Carmina looked over at Sherlock, smiling.

"What's with the smile?"

"It's just that now is when I realize, we both think people are assholes."

Sherlock laughed.

"Why do you think I spend most of my time with Thor?"

He pointed at his furry companion, who was sound asleep next to him on the truck bench seat, conserving his energy, no doubt, for the investigation.

Chapter 16

Watson was standing over Ripshaw. The sack that was once over the Plague Doctor's head was now gripped in the English detective's hand.

"I am going to remove this rag from your mouth, Ripshaw. Do not scream; if you do, the rag goes right back in. Do you understand?"

Ripshaw stared at Watson, who wore the crow mask and looked very menacing, looking back at him. He nodded in agreement.

Watson tossed the sack he was holding on the floor and walked over to the tied-up Ripshaw. He reached out with one hand and pulled down the rag, as the Plague Doctor wiggled his mouth free the rest of the way.

"You fucking asshole. Take that mask off."

The demand seemed to come from a place of possession more than of fear.

"Why should I? Does it belong to you?"

This was Watson's way of making him admit that he was who Carmen said he was. It would be the only way that John Watson could kill another man, knowing that he caused death and destruction to others, would justify murdering him.

Instead, Ripshaw played innocent.

"Keep the mask on for all I care. What the fuck is the meaning of this anyway? Why did you attack me?"

Ripshaw was trying to catch his breath from being gagged and having his head bagged.

"Well, you see, Ripshaw, it's like this: I have been given information that leads me to believe you are the Plague Doctor. Descended from a line of individuals who have caused massive amounts of sickness and pain."

Ripshaw blurted out a laugh that held an edge of confidence to it.

"I don't know where you have received your information from, Dr. Watson, but it is absolute bullshit."

"Tell me, Ripshaw, what kind of doctor are you?"

"You think I owe you an explanation for my capture? Fuck you."

This angered Watson; wearing that crow mask made his soul feel dark, powerful, and primal.

"You will tell me what I want to know, Ripshaw, one way or another."

The tied-up Plague Doctor said nothing; instead, he spat at Watson's feet.

"Very well, time to play."

Watson walked over to the motel telephone, disconnected the curly cord from the base and the receiver, setting the receiver down. He walked behind Ripshaw, placed the telephone cord around his neck, pulling it tight.

Ripsaw began squirming and coughing in the chair, his breath being pulled out by his neck thanks to Watson.

Watson didn't recognize himself torturing this man, but he couldn't resist the urge to continue.

"Answer me, Ripshaw, tell me what you did."

Ripshaw continued to struggle; his eyes began bulging as he attempted to gasp for every inch of breath he could get.

Watson continued choking him with the telephone cord for a few more seconds and then released the cord from around Ripsaw's neck.

He coughed, shook his head vigorously, attempting to snap out of being choked alive.

Between breaths, he continued his denial of the things he had done.

"I didn't do anything wrong."

The Plague Doctor huffed out of his mouth, which made Watson smile.

"Let's continue to play, then, shall we?"

"Play what, you piece of shit? This isn't a game; you are torturing me."

"Dear Ripshaw, that is the game. How much of this am I going to have to do before you tell me the truth? Just tell me, and I'll make the pain stop."

"Fuck…you."

Watson nodded. He held the telephone cord from one end and began whipping Ripshaw's face with it. Whip, after whip, after whip.

The phone cord left slash marks on his face, matching the curved line on his neck, courtesy of Dr. John Watson.

"You must know, things will only progress from here."

Watson felt an urge to become even more creative with his torture methods. Still, he justified the torture in his mind. Torturing someone was better than killing them, at least that part of his conscience still functioned, for now.

Ripshaw grimaced with every slash, then he muttered something that slightly tipped his hand of information.

"That bitch must have sent you."

Watson stopped whipping and tossed the phone cord onto the floor, not far from the bag that was on his victim's head.

"The bitch? What bitch might that be?"

Of course, Watson knew the answer, but he wanted Ripshaw to say Carmen's name.

He stayed silent and glared at his torturer.

"No answer? Good, I was hoping you would want to continue our game."

The detective looked around the motel room to get creative about what other tools he could use to extract information from the Plague Doctor.

Then the metal antenna sticking out from behind the motel television caught his attention. He smiled, walked over to the TV, and broke off one of the antennas.

Watson walked back over to Ripshaw, as they stared at each other in a tense moment. The crow-masked doctor Watson then started sliding the antenna point up Ripsaw's nose. He screamed in horror, feeling the metal pole slide up his nostril; he could feel as if it reached deep behind his sinus cavity.

"Okay, okay, I'll talk."

The agony of pain made his voice quiver to get the words out.

Pleased, yet somewhat disappointed that his game would not continue, Watson slid the antenna out of the nostril, and a slight spec of blood was visible on the round antenna end.

"I want to know what you did and everything you can tell me about the La Lechuza organization."

"I have been with the organization for a long time. I only did what they told me to do."

"Which was what? Tell me what you did, Ripshaw."

"Whenever they asked me to create illnesses to make someone disappear and look like an accident, I did it. Sometimes things would get out of hand, and there was collateral damage."

"Go on."

Watson knew there was so much more; he intended to find out every part of it.

"Politicians, movie stars, lawyers, businesspeople, you name it, I did it."

"Yet you never asked why they wanted you to kill these people through illnesses or poison?"

"It wasn't my job to question them, Watson; they would do to me far worse than what you are doing to me right now."

"But it didn't end there, did it, Ripshaw? You hurt more people than that."

Ripshaw huffed, and blood began trickling from his nose onto his lap.

"Yes, I did. I had to experiment on people to make sure that those sicknesses I was creating worked."

"Who did you test it on, Ripshaw?"

The anger in Dr. Watson's voice was growing more tense, awaiting the answer he expected to hear.

"The old, the young, everyone in between. You would be shocked at how easy it is to access a city's water system. It was some of my best work."

The smugness on display took Watson back a little, but he was able to conceal his discontent under the mask.

"How deep does La Lechuza run?"

Ripshaw bellowed a laugh.

"You have no fucking idea, do you? Do you even know who you work for?"

"I don't work for them; I am just an associate."

Watson clarified, attempting to distance himself from the secret society.

"Is that what you think? Oh, John, you're in over your head and don't even know it. It is a centuries-old witches' coven. They have eyes everywhere, and the moment someone goes against what they want, they eliminate them. Hence, your presence here."

"Tell me more." Watson sat at the end of the bed, keeping a reasonable distance away from Ripshaw.

"They control ungodly creatures. La Lechuza got its name from an entity that has the head of a woman and the body of an owl. Folklore tells that La Lechuza would punish those it deemed wicked. Yet that is the fuzzy part, how they determine who is good and who is evil is completely arbitrary."

"I don't know, they seem to be right about you. By your own admission, you harmed innocent people. You don't seem remorseful about it, and in fact, you seem like a liability. So, were they wrong about you?"

The Plague Doctor looked down at the ground, then returned his gaze towards Watson.

"I regret nothing, in the name of science, the weak must sacrifice for the strong. So, some people died, fuck them. Their lives served a greater purpose. I come from a long line of Plague Doctors, and I wore that mask, which you have no honor to wear, for a long time. My work is noble."

Watson stood up from the bed and approached Ripshaw.

"Tell me, is murder noble?"

"It is for the right reasons, Watson, yes."

Watson nodded, produced a revolver tucked behind his waistband, and shot Ripshaw in the eye socket. With one loud BANG, smoke still coming from the barrel of the pistol, Ripshaw's head jerked back, blood splattered behind him on the floor and wall. The shot caused instant death. The eye socket began gushing warm blood that streamed down Ripshaw's face.

"I am the most noble person you will know."

Watson stated to the corpse of Ripshaw.

Chapter 17

Laney just returned to work after her encounter with the Mothman. Though she cleaned herself up, she could still feel the heat of his warm cum that landed on her. As she started her shift, Bubba Chance, her boss and the owner of the burger joint, approached her.

"We need to talk in my office."

Laney rolled her eyes, knowing she was going to be lectured on being late for work. Bubba Chance was typically an asshole to his employees.

She followed him to the back of the restaurant while she was tying her white waist apron around herself. They reached the office door. Bubba opened it and gestured for Laney to go inside, which she did.

The office was cold, with some photos of cars hanging on the walls, except for the one hanging by a corner of the frame that his lazy ass never bothered to fix.

She heard the door lock behind her. Ever since she began messing around with Vlad, she felt her senses heightened.

Bubba walked around her and stood in front of his desk. He did not offer her a seat, nor did he let her sit down on his green vinyl chair, the same one she interviewed in.

"Look here, I didn't want to tell you this in front of the rest of the staff, but you've been screwing up lately. I caught you skipping out during your shift the other day, which I am docking from your next paycheck."

She offered no excuses. She just figured if she stayed quiet long enough, she would not have to hear anymore of his bullshit.

"Today, you came in late. If you want this job, you must take some responsibility. I want you here on time and not leaving anymore during work hours."

Laney nodded at Bubba and tried to look apologetic, though the truth is, she wouldn't change getting her pussy eaten by the Mothman for anything in the world.

"Do you understand me, Laney?"

His voice was stern, with a gruff edge.

"Yes, Mr. Chance, I will make sure it won't happen again."

She delivered that line convincingly, she thought, even if it was complete bullshit.

"That's good, Laney."

Bubba motioned for Laney to leave. As she turned around to walk towards the front door, she could hear his steps behind her.

He grabbed her right ass cheek, rubbing his hand over her.

Laney was taken aback. She spun around quickly to see Bubba's big gut and grinning, toothy smile looking at her.

"What the fuck are you doing?"

"Don't you talk to your boss that way. Next time you are late, we are going to come right back to this office and bend that plump, round ass of yours over my chair, and I'll teach you a lesson."

Laney felt rage; she was frozen, caught off guard. This scumbag tried to strip her of the confidence, power, and bravery she had felt with one gesture.

"Don't you touch me ever again?"

She demanded with a growl.

"Look here, girlie, I know it's just you and your aunt and that you need this job. So, you will do what I say when I say it; if not, you and your aunt will be out on your asses in no time without any money coming in."

Her heart burned with rage, hellfire running through her veins. Her initial thought was to deck him, but she felt like that wouldn't have been enough.

Bubba Chance got close to her, a few inches from her face. She could feel his hot, disgusting breath on her.

"I won't take no for an answer."

Laney was fumbling with the door lock behind her back, finally getting it open. She ran out of the office, running into a waitress carrying a tray of food. They both fell to the ground. With a loud crash, everything on the tray fell to the restaurant floor. The burgers, the shakes, the fries…everything.

The restaurant stopped, and everyone looked at Laney. Bubba Chance, who was walking out of his office, looked at the floor decorated with all the food he would now have to pay to replace to complete those orders.

He was livid; he glared at Laney as she pulled herself up and helped the other waitress to stand as well.

"I'm sorry."

Laney muttered to the waitress she knocked over.

"That's strike three, girlie."

Bubba was aching to get her into his office to take advantage of her.

Laney went to the bathroom to gain her composure. She was furious, she looked in the mirror, makeup running down her face from tears, she was fighting back while she was being sexually harassed.

She looked up at the mirror; she didn't like what she saw looking back at her: a victim, someone who was overpowered by a situation she did not expect or ask for.

"No fucking way am I going to let this slide."

She said it to herself in the mirror and out loud so she could hear it. No way was this dominant female going to let some piece of shit ever treat her like that. If she could command a winged demon to her sexual urges, she could surely control anyone else, she thought.

At that moment, Laney had a glorious idea.

She wiped off the smeared makeup, fixed her hair, and straightened her posture. She walked outside of the ladies' bathroom and straight to Bubba's office.

"Hey, Mr. Chance, will you give me a ride home today?"

"Oh, I'll give you a ride, alright, glad you are coming to your senses. I'll take you home...the long way."

He winked at her, she returned a forced smile, then she exited his office.

She knew she had to work her shift; in a few hours, she would have to deal with Bubba Chance's unwanted sexual advancements again.

Chapter 18

As Laney was finishing her shift, Bubba approached her.

"Get your stuff together, I have Carl closing tonight. Time for me to give you that ride you promised me."

Laney let out a sigh.

"Yes, I'm ready. We must come back here to get my aunt's car afterwards so I can drive it home."

"Don't worry, I'll bring you back."

They entered Bubba's Hudson Hornet car.

She wasted no time trying to take control of the situation.

"I know a quiet spot we could go to. Just down the highway at the edge of town."

"Oh yeah? Is that where all the young people go to fuck?"

"Kind of."

She shrugged to play as if being coy.

"Okay, tell me which way to go."

After a few brief directions, Bubba was driving down the highway. The exact route Laney had taken earlier in the evening.

"Now listen, when we get there, you do what I say. I don't want any back talk, you understand?"

"Yes, Mr. Chance."

Laney smiled with an internal gloat.

"Call me Bubba, after all, we are about to get very familiar with one another." Bubba rolled a toothpick from one side of his mouth to the other side.

"Okay, Bubba. Slow down, when you get to this opening in the pines, turn onto that dirt road."

Bubba followed her instructions and brought the Hudson to a slow stop. He turned down the dirt road. After a few turns, Laney told him to stop the car.

"This is the spot. Turn the car off."

"Alright, now we're talking."

He grabbed the key and turned off the ignition, then looked at Laney and tried to slide closer to her.

"Wait, not here."

She placed her hand on his hairy chest.

"What the fuck do you mean not here?"

"I mean, let's do it outside, we need more space."

"Oh yeah, we do, I like that thinking girlie."

They both exited their respective doors and walked toward the front of the car.

"Bend over the hood so I can lift your skirt."

She turned to face the car and put her palms on the hood.

"Good girl."

Before he could reach down to grab the end of her skirt, she shouted out to the night sky.

"Come out of your corner, Vlad, your madam commands you."

"What the fuck are you talking about? Shut up and put your head down, would'ya?"

The thump that landed on the ground behind Bubba was loud, and the soil shook a little under his feet.

Bubba Chance spun around and stared at this massive, winged creature with ruby red bulging eyes.

"What the fuck is that?"

Bubba's voice sounded shaky.

"Vlad, I brought you a gift. A feast just for you to thank you for being a good boy to your madam."

"You said no more killing."

Mothman's voice was as smooth as silk nestled in her ears.

"Killing? You can't let this monster kill me?! I'll fucking end you bitch."

"Feed my love, feed when I tell you to."

Mothman stepped towards Bubba. With one fluid motion, he grabbed Bubba by the throat and began to squeeze. Bubba's face immediately began turning a blueish-purple color while his feet began to lift off the ground.

"Squeeze him harder."

Laney hissed with a tone that was filled with bloodlust and passion.

Mothman obeyed, and his claws dug deeper into Bubba's neck; blood began to seep out. Vlad opened his mouth, fangs extended, puncturing Bubba's neck from the opposite side that was being held. He began slurping the blood from his meal, draining whatever life force was left in the restaurant owner.

The blood dripped from the Mothman's lips, cascading to the ground below him, saturating the soil with the warm blood of what used to be Bubba Chance.

Laney's face wore a wide-eyed smile; the sight of this killing enthralled her. It turned her on, and she wanted more.

"Vlad, come to me."

The Mothman tossed Bubba Chance to the ground, his body collapsing like a sack of potatoes. Bubba's arm hit the front hood of the Hudson as his lifeless body fell.

He moved towards Laney. She tossed her hair and walked past him into the darker parts of the woods.

"Follow me, Vlad."

"Yes, my dear Laney."

They walked deeper into the woods, where the darkness allowed her eyes to adjust. She leaned against a solid pine tree and stared up at her winged sex slave.

Looking up at Mothman's glowing red eyes, she couldn't help but feel her chest heaving up and down as her breath caught in excitement. Mothman looked at her beautiful breasts that were threatening to burst out of her dress.

Laney reached under her dress and pulled off her black panties as Vlad watched intently. She bunched them up in her hand and reached for Mothman's clawed hand, placing them in his. He squeezed her panties tight in his grip. She turned around and wrapped her arms around the tree as wide as she could and leaned her ass out.

"Take me, Vlad, take your mistress right now."

Mothman's two-headed cock came out of the feather grouping in his mid-section. She could feel her dress lifting, the night air hitting her plump ass cheeks. He moved his claws over the shoulder of her dress and slid both sides of her dress and bra down, exposing more of her upper back and neck.

Vlad gently bit her shoulder, causing her legs to go weak with lust. She moaned as his forked tongue licked up her neck and ear. She could feel her pussy was dripping wet from his touch.

"I want you, Laney. I want every inch of your skin, of your touch. My cock yearns for you."

"Give it to me, Vlad."

She said, her voice trailing off, as she enjoyed her monster's touch.

"I said, give it to me!"

Now she commanded it, and Vlad was happy to oblige.

He slid one of his cock heads into her soft and warm pussy. He was gentle, allowing her lips to receive his cock slowly, allowing her natural moisture to lubricate his cock with every inch that began passing into her. It was her first time having sex; her body squirmed slightly with the first few thrusts as slight discomfort turned into ecstasy.

Mothman grabbed her hips from both sides and began pulling her pussy even deeper into him. She moaned as she gripped the bark of the tree.

Laney began backing her ass into Vlad, taking control. Though he was behind her, she was in control and pumping into him. He passed his claw over her back, making scratch marks. With every burn of the marks he made on her, she thrusted into him harder. His wings expanded in a chorus of pleasure. The pop of his wings expanding allowed his cock to lift while in her pussy, raising her feet off the ground slightly.

He was hitting the right spot; he gnarled, hissed, and moaned as they both created a chorus of passion and fucking sounds that echoed through the woods.

Her pussy was dripping from his cock onto the ground. She was amazed how he was able to put one cock head into her, then she felt the second one slide in, stretching her pussy in just the right way.

"Fuck me, slave, fuck me until I tell you to stop."

Mothman listened to his master's command, continuing to fuck her.

"Those feel so good in me."

"Yes, my queen."

****

"She feels magnificent, her pussy is hugging both my heads, she is amazing."

Mothman reached over Laney's mouth and stuffed the panties she gave him into it. He gagged her with her own panties; she bit down on them, giving out muffled moans.

"I wonder how she would like it if I slapped her ass?"

Slap!

The sound of his clawed hand hitting her ass cheek made her fucking feel that much more primal. Her inhibitions with him were disappearing.

"Harder."

She growled out through her panties that were clenched in her teeth.

"That's it, command me, my queen, I will give you this cock just the way you want it."

Slap!

He slapped her ass again, slightly harder than the first time, leaving a red mark on her lovely, tanned skin.

Reaching below her, he clawed off the top of her dress, as her tits hung down, and he squeezed them both.

He placed both his clawed hands on her shoulders, pulling her back to him, causing her tits to slap against her body. The sound turned Vlad on even more, fluttering his wings, making the leaves in the trees around them sway with the breeze he created. His forked tongue licked her neck and earlobe as he slid in and out of her warm pussy.

"I have never felt a woman this good. My cocks feel so welcomed in her; my cocks were made for her."

Laney shook her head from side to side with the panties hanging out of her mouth. The thrusting made her teeth lose their grip slightly.

"Her back is tensing, she is going to cum, I can feel it. Her thighs are tightening; her back is arching. That sweet nectar is going to squirt out again."

Just as he knew she was going to cum, she announced it for her slave.

"I'm cumming, slave!"

Just as Laney's pussy began to squirt, Mothman removed himself from her, dropped to his muscular knees, and placed his mouth right under her. She squirted into his mouth as he lapped it up with his forked tongue, going into her pussy walls to suck as much of her sweet juice as he could.

"Oh, Vlad, drink it all like a good boy."

She said to him in her mistress's command voice through clenched panty teeth.

As Mothman was drinking and sucking Laney's pussy, the excitement of having his queen caused him to cum, while he was on his knees. His seed shot out to the forest floor.

Her body quivered from squirting and climaxing so hard.

"Yes, her body is vibrating. Let every drop of your nectar slide down my tongue, my queen."

Her body was completely relaxed; she did not smoke cigarettes. If Laney had been smoking, this would have been the time to do it.

Once Vlad drank all the juice from her, he stood up. She turned around, removing the panties from her mouth.

They embraced; she could feel his feathery chest against her face.

Then, she released him, embodying her full master role.

"What do you say to your master?"

Mothman got down on one knee and bowed his head.

"Thank you for your sweet nectar, my queen."

"You were a good boy. Now we must clean up this mess. People at work saw me leaving with that piece of shit I gifted you."

"I will clean this mess, my queen."

"I need to get back home somehow, and I can't drive his car back."

Mothman stood up and wrapped his strong gray arms around her.

"I can take you back."

Laney pulled her dress top back on and pulled down the bottom part of her dress.

Laney held him around his waist tightly, and he fluttered his wings up, lifting them both off the ground. She was in awe as she saw herself rising above the branches of the trees and the forest. She left her panties on the ground, appreciating the cool air that was hitting her pussy as Mothman began flying her towards town.

"It is the dark of night; we will go fast enough that no one will see you."

"Drop me off in my backyard. I will tell you how to get there."

"No need, my master, I already know where you live."

Laney looked at Vlad and smiled.

"Bad boy, but I will let it slide tonight."

Laney was developing a plan as Mothman flew her through the night sky.

Her story would be that Bubba gave her a ride home because she had car trouble. After that, she never saw him again. After all, no one would believe poor ole' Laney would be capable of harming another person. Shows how little they knew of her, Laney got a taste of blood and fucking in her system, she was not about to allow either of those strong traits subside.

As they both traveled over Point Pleasant, satisfied, Laney was content that she got her justice over the creep she worked for and lost her virginity to her sexual creature on the same night.

Chapter 19

Mothman landed gently in the backyard of Laney's aunt's house. The grass provided a gentle spot to land slowly. Laney did not want to let go of Vlad's embrace, but she knew she had to.

"Thank you for bringing me home."

Mothman smiled at her, wiping away a blood droplet from her face that splattered when he choked the life out of Bubba Chance and squeezed him like an orange.

"You are very welcome. I will take care of the scene we left behind."

"I will tell anyone who asks that he left me home, drove off from here. My assumption is he went home, and I do not know what happened from there."

Laney stared adoringly at her creature slave. She wanted to command him more, to fuck her from behind, to eat her pussy, to ravage her as she commanded, but she quickly remembered that there was a corpse to be dealt with, and she had to go inside to ensure her aunt saw that she was home as part of her cover story.

She walked up to him and placed two fingers in his mouth. She had to raise her arm higher because of his height, which she estimated at around 6'6.

Vlad stared at her and sucked her fingers, passing his forked tongue over both. She then removed her fingers from his mouth, sliding them into her own.

"Good Mothy."

She turned around to head into the house when she had another sexually diabolical idea.

"Wait here."

She commanded Vlad in an eager tone.

Laney walked past him into the metal storage shed that was in the backyard. She slid the rusty metal door open, walking into the darkness. Vlad just stared at the shed opening as he took a few curious steps towards where he last saw her enter.

After a few brief moments, Mothman could see Laney's curvy figure standing at the shed door, holding something in her hands.

His master stepped out of the darkness with a heavy metal dog chain hanging from her hand.

She approached Mothman with a sultry smile.

"We will put these chains around your neck; it's a symbol. This means, you belong to me, you do as your master tells you, understood?"

Mothman kneeled in front of Laney. She placed the chain around his neck and used the metal clip to connect it. The chain was used by her aunt when she tried to keep a stray dog; the animal escaped, but this one won't.

Once the chain was clipped, Laney grabbed the end of it and pulled it towards her. She was facing Mothman, red eyes in full bloom. She stared at his lips. He retracted his fangs.

Finally, after all their fucking, she wanted her romantic kiss with her monster. Their lips collided in a passionate embrace. She could feel the leather of his smooth lips; he could feel the soft poutiness of hers, the same trait that drove him wild when she had him in her mouth.

Vlad moved his tongue into her mouth, and she caressed his with hers until their faces were in a full kissing session.

Laney moved back, staring at each other. She placed her hands on both sides of his face, looking deep to see if she could recognize a human in those eyes.

Vlad placed his claw-like hands on hers, slowly moving them away.

"I have always been a monster in one way or another, but now, I am your monster, Laney."

"Don't you ever fucking forget it."

She said, smiling, as all the joy in her heart wanted to explode into a thousand pieces like fireworks. Except she wouldn't, the last two times she exploded, Mothman drank her natural juices when she squirted into his mouth.

"Go now, I will see you soon."

Laney walked past Vlad. By the time she turned around, he was gone.

Laney entered her aunt's house through the front door. Her aunt was perceptive and would have noticed Laney coming in from the back, so she made the effort to walk around the side of the house, unlatch the wood gate, and enter through the front door.

"Laney, I didn't hear the car in the driveway."

"Yeah, the boss at work, Bubba, gave me a ride because the car didn't start."

"Oh, I'm sorry about that. Sometimes when the weather gets colder, it acts up. Maybe we can ask Jordie for a ride to the burger joint tomorrow, and I could give it a try? I swear sometimes that car only works for me."

"Sounds great, Tia. I am going to go to bed; it's been a long day at work."

As Laney walked up the stairs, her aunt felt something was different about Laney, but she couldn't quite figure out what it was just yet.

Chapter 20

Sherlock and Carmina had good timing on their trip; they arrived in Roanoke, Virginia, just in time to find a place to stay for the night.

"Where do you recommend we stay?"

"There are plenty of motels in the area. We could get a room to rest up."

Carmina sounded sure of her plan, very matter-of-fact. They had made small talk on their road trip. Sherlock told her about some of his old cases, and Carmina educated Sherlock on cryptids he had never heard of.

"Just the one room, Carmina? People may talk."

Sherlock gave her a charming grin.

"Let them talk, besides Sherlock, not to hurt your feelings, but you aren't really my type."

"Really? I thought my old-world British charisma was everyone's type."

"Not mine, but you are charming."

"So, tell me, Carmina, what is your type?"

Carmina leaned back on her driver's chair, gripping the steering wheel with one hand. She gave out a loud laugh and smiled.

"Sherlock, I like my women with fur and a snout. Does that answer your question?"

"You like dogs?"

"Don't be an asshole, Sherlock. I like wolves, specifically female werewolves."

"Werewolf, you say. Well, paint me intrigued."

Carmina shook her head in a manner that meant she was not going to have this conversation now.

"Save it for another day, Sherlock."

Sherlock could see this was emotional territory that he did not want to traverse. After a few moments of silence, Carmina spoke up.

"Let's stop here at this motel, Croatoan."

The Motel Croatoan was named after the word carved into a tree's bark, which marked the disappearance of a group of settlers in 1590. The inscription was the only evidence found that people inhabited the area at the time when a search party could not locate the English colony.

The peach-colored motel building had a white car porch awning so people could pull up to the front door to check in. The words "Motel Croatoan" were on a baby-blue neon sign with the letter M blinking. The building's colors clashed with the neon words, like a sand sandwich.

Sherlock and Carmina exited the vehicle with Thor in tow and made their way to the front door. Sherlock held the door open for Carmina; she nodded as they both entered.

When they arrived at the front desk, no one was there. A radio with swing music was playing in the background.

A glance around, Sherlock could see that the two lobby chairs had dust on them. A sign that individuals have not been visiting or certainly not hanging out in the hotel lobby.

A sign written in black ink gave directions to those who needed assistance.

"Ring the bell for help."

Carmina did just that; she tapped the top of the round metal bell on the counter, which rang. She hit the button three or four times in fast succession.

Finally, someone emerged from the back office. It was a short man. He was so vertically challenged in stature that by Sherlock's estimate, he could not have been more than 4 feet. The man walked along a ramp built behind the counter, which elevated him several feet so he could see people from a higher vantage point.

The man had a beard; he was bald, with menacing, bushy eyebrows.

"How can I help you?"

"We need a room with two beds, please."

Carmina smiled as the motel employee moved his glances between Sherlock and Carmina, attempting to determine the nature of their relationship.

"Um, okay. Well, I have a room available. Nightly rate is eight dollars; you pay upfront."

The man's voice had the smoothness of a chainsaw. Though the motel did not seem to be a five-star resort, it would do for one night.

Sherlock reached into his coat pocket and pulled out his brown leather billfold. He presented the man with ten dollars in cash.

The man seemed annoyed by this. In part, he very much gave the impression that he did not want to be bothered by guests.

"I don't have change to give you."

"No worries, my good sir, you keep the additional two dollars as a tip for your sunny disposition."

The sarcasm was as gentle as it could be. Carmina smirked at Sherlock's wit.

"The two dollars are for a pet fee; just make sure he doesn't pee on the carpet."

Thor looked at the motel man, growling, not appreciating the insinuation that he would urinate on carpets. For the record, he absolutely does.

Then, Sherlock saw something that caught his eye. Something that he found a little unsettling. Behind the counter was a picture on the wall of a woman's head on an owl's body. He had seen this image before in his travels and asked Watson to find information about the symbol's meaning. He never received a straight answer to his inquiry from Watson.

Of course, he was unaware that Carmina was a member of the society represented by that symbol; he thought she was a monster/cryptid enthusiast.

Sherlock's past attempts to inquire had led nowhere. So, he decided on a different tactic.

"I want you to know, I am familiar with that symbol."

The motel man had a confused look on his face.

He stared at Sherlock up and down, then he looked in Carmina's direction.

"No, you aren't." The reply was fast, almost instinctual from the man.

"What makes you say that? As a matter of fact, I have a friend who works in a train station in New York that sports the same symbol."

This was Sherlock's attempt at bullshit; he did meet someone who worked in a train station who wore a pin with that symbol, but it was no friend of Sherlock's.

"That's a nice story, mister. Here is your room key, number 12."

"May I ask your name, sir?"

"My name is Champ. Now, if there isn't anything else, I'll see you at check-out tomorrow morning, 9 a.m. sharp."

"Time to go, Sherlock, I'm sleepy. Thank you for your time, Champ."

Champ nodded at Carmina; she ushered the inquisitive detective towards the front door. Then, right before he opened the glass door for Carmina, he had one more question for Champ.

"Curious, Mr. Champ, do you get visitors very often?"

Champ smiled at him, pointing his finger at Sherlock.

"You would be the first one from England who hasn't disappeared."

"Indeed, goodnight, Mr. Champ."

Sherlock and Carmina made their exit, a brief sigh of relief that the questioning of the motel man had ended.

"Alright, Sherlock, we will be up bright and early, and by tomorrow, we will be in Point Pleasant so that you can investigate your monster."

"I can hardly wait, Carmina."

Sherlock and Carmina made their way into their motel room. Once there, Sherlock removed his coat and hat as Carmina brought down her duffel bag from the car.

"Oh, I need to get my bag from the car."

Sherlock used this excuse to go outside and then return to the front desk for more information, no matter how annoyed Champ was.

"Go ahead, I am going to shower and get ready for bed. I am tired from the long drive."

She tossed the car keys to Sherlock.

"Lock the car when you're done."

Carmina walked towards the bathroom, closing the door behind her. Once Sherlock heard the shower run, he exited the room. Then he walked back towards the front desk of the motel.

Thor was placed on one of the beds and made himself comfortable.

He could see there was someone else behind the counter this time, a blonde woman with fair skin. He intended to go back to the front desk, further poking around. He was curious about the motel, the employee, and the symbol on the wall: an owl's body with a woman's face.

As he walked in, the woman behind the counter greeted Sherlock warmly. She sported the same stature as the man, maybe a few inches taller. He was struck by how attractive she was; he estimated she could not have been more than thirty-five years old.

"May I help you?"

"Yes, I am your guest in room 12. By the looks of the parking lot, we may be your only guests tonight."

The woman gave a brief chuckle, appreciating Sherlock's joke.

"You are not wrong. We don't get many visitors here, at least not at this time of the year."

They exchanged flirtatious glances.

"What can I assist you with?"

"Well, we will be checking out tomorrow, and I wanted to know of a good place to get breakfast in the area."

Small talk is his way of breaking down verbal barriers, allowing people to let their guard down when they speak with him. However, he appreciates the company of the pretty lady.

"Well, in town, there is the Nightcrawler Diner. It's pretty good food, and a damn good cup of coffee if I do say so myself."

"Thank you, that was very helpful. I'm Sherlock, what's your name?"

"I'm Huldra."

Sherlock noted that her name was of Scandinavian origin.

"A Pleasure to make your acquaintance. When I checked in earlier, I met your father, perhaps?"

"Oh, Champ, not my father, he's my brother. Generally, a grouch, I hope he wasn't too rude towards you."

"Nothing you couldn't make up to me with the pleasure of your company."

Sherlock was a bit smitten. Though Huldra was shorter than the women he was used to, he absolutely appreciated that about her. To Sherlock, different is beautiful.

"My, Mr. Sherlock, are you hitting on me?"

Sherlock casually leaned on the counter.

"If I were, would that be so terrible?"

"You are cute, Sherlock, but honestly, I don't think you could handle the ride."

"Only one way to find out, Huldra."

Huldra was as blunt as a bulldozer; she could sniff out a cheap come-on line from any guy. Except, this felt different, a little daring and forbidden.

"How long are you staying with us, Mr. Sherlock?"

"Just the one night."

"So, what do you think is going to happen. You flirt with me, I take you to an empty room, and fuck your brains out? Because you think that the slightest attention to a little woman, she will do anything with any guy?"

Sherlock felt a bit embarrassed; he felt as if he had insulted Huldra. It was not his intent; he really was attracted to her.

"I am so sorry, Huldra, I meant no offense. You are a beautiful woman; I thought a compliment with a touch of flirting was healthy. I truly apologize."

"Apologize? Why? Now you don't think I'm pretty?"

Sherlock was confused; did he say something wrong by apologizing? Even his detective skills weren't enough to decipher what Huldra was getting at.

"I am not sure what to say."

He slightly stuttered, partly out of nervousness.

Huldra began to laugh loudly.

"That was too easy. I was fucking with you, Sherlock. Meet me in room 5 in twenty minutes."

"Really?"

Sherlock couldn't hide his excitement.

"Look, you are a man, I'm a woman. You think men are the only ones that like to fuck?"

"I hope not," Sherlock said with a laugh.

"Twenty minutes, room 5. The door will be unlocked."

Sherlock reached for her hand, grabbed it, and kissed it. He enjoyed how soft her hand was when he grabbed it.

"I can hardly wait."

Sherlock exited the hotel lobby. He walked towards the car and opened the trunk. He took out his small luggage bag and closed the trunk. Then he ensured the vehicle was closed correctly.

When he walked in, Carmina was sitting up in bed reading a book.

"What are you reading?"

"Just something I brought along with me. Are you familiar with the art of Necromancy?"

"I am aware of the meaning of the word."

"Well then, that answers your question."

"Look, Carmina, I need to step out for a little while."

Carmina did not like this; she needed to keep tabs on Sherlock.

"Where the fuck are you going to go at this time?"

"Oh, I don't need to borrow the car. You see, I met a woman, I have a date, of sorts."

"Sherlock, we have been here less than an hour, how the hell do you have a date?"

"I went back to the front desk."

Carmina immediately looked annoyed.

He put up his hands in a surrender gesture.

"I know, I know, this time in the front lobby, there was a woman. Turns out she is Champ's sister. She is my date tonight."

"Where are you two going to go?"

"If I am lucky, all the way."

"I will see you in the morning, Sherlock."

He smiled. Petted Thor, reassuring him he would return, then he left.

Chapter 21

Watson had sat in the motel room for a while thinking of what he had done. He had killed another man. It wasn't like when he was in the British Navy, when sometimes his orders were to take out enemy ships. This was a man who did wrong and admitted it. That was the justification Watson gave himself for killing him.

It was a few hours, and night had fallen on the town of Twain, Georgia. There was a knock on his motel door; he was hoping it was Carmina.

Watson looked through the peephole and saw three men in black suits standing outside the door.

He opened the door so that only a sliver of his face showed, blocking the view inside the motel room, where a dead body sat lifeless and bloody in a chair.

"Yes?"

He was not expecting company, especially not three men who looked official.

"Dr. John Watson?"

"Yes, that is correct. How can I help you?"

"We are associates of La Lechuza, Carmen asked us to come."

Watson could see the pins on all their lapels—a gold owl, with the head of a woman.

"Tell Carmen I did what she asked."

"We are aware of that, Dr. Watson. That is why we are here, to assist you in your cleaning efforts."

"Oh, I see."

"Could you please open the door fully?"

"Of course, please come in."

The three men, who did not offer their names, stood looking at Ripshaw's body.

"Very well done, Dr. Watson. We can handle things from here."

The person who seemed to be in charge handed Watson a room key.

"This is the key to room 104. That will be your new accommodation for your stay."

Watson grabbed the key, looking at the men, wondering how they knew he had already killed his target.

Watson nodded in understanding and took the room key offered to him.

"Oh, Dr. Watson, one more thing."

The leader of the group of men leaned over the bed and picked up the crow-designed black Plague Doctor mask, handing it to Watson.

"Carmen says this belongs to you now. I would take it if I were you, Dr. Watson."

Watson grabbed the mask.

"Your belongings will be taken to your room shortly."

He felt like a contract killer, someone who did the dirty deed for others. This wasn't his fight. Was the killing righteous? In his mind, he tried to convince himself it was.

After grabbing the mask, Watson began walking out of the room. Then he turned back towards the men.

"I want to talk to Carmen, right now!" It was a demand, the demand of a man who wanted more answers.

"We will certainly convey your message to her. Currently, she is in New Jersey, dealing with her own devils."

With that very vague reassurance, Watson walked out of the motel room as he heard the door slam closed behind him.

Chapter 22

After Laney was safe at home, Mothman returned to the scene of his thrashing of Bubba Chance. There was blood that had already brought around other animals, specifically a large, primal wolf. The wolf was gnawing on the body, licking up whatever was left of the blood Vlad did not drink.

"Well, haven't seen you in a while."

The wolf gave Mothman a thousand-yard stare, licked her chomp, then growled.

"Easy now, let's not rehash old grievances. By all means, eat up as much as you like."

The wolf got back to eating the remains of the gritty burger hop owner.

"Now, what do we do about this car? Hiding it suggests something suspicious. No, this car needs to be found."

Mothman moved past the wolf. He walked over to the car door, opened it with his claw hand, then reached in, grabbed the gearshift, and put the car in neutral. He then walked to the front of the vehicle and pushed it back from the hood. His strength was impressive; the car, though heavy, seemed to move easily through the woods, making sounds as it hit various branches.

The chain Laney had placed around his neck hung slightly, hitting his gray chest as he pushed the car.

He pushed it straight back until the vehicle was almost at the road. The trunk sticking out of the woods would let people know he veered off the highway.

Satisfied that the car would be noticed, he moved back towards the woods. He could not stop thinking of Laney. Wanting her, he remembered how earlier in the night, his claws could feel the beautiful, plumped folds of her skin as he thrusted himself deeper into her.

Once he returned, the wolf had taken part of the carcass with it and dragged it deep into the forest of West Virginia. Some organs, blood, and flesh remained on the ground. Vlad decided to leave it there. It would be proof that a wild animal ate him. What would still be unclear is why, after driving off the road, Bubba Chance would have gone into the woods?

That part of the story had to be cleaned up, but he also figured it would drive the constables in town crazy as they tried to figure it out.

With that done, Mothman went back to the tree that his master told him to stay in.

Chapter 23

Sherlock walked up to the door of room number 5. He straightened his wool vest, rolled up his white Stafford shirt sleeve, and then knocked on the door. He remembered that Huldra had told him the room would be unlocked. He stopped mid-knock and turned the handle to open the door.

The door opened, allowing Sherlock to enter the room. Huldra was already there, standing on top of the queen-size bed. Other than one bed instead of two, the room looked exactly like his, except for the wall art. In room 5, the art featured different versions of a half-naked woman caressing wolves.

There was only one light on, the lamp on the nightstand next to the bed.

"Well, hello, Sherlock, come here."

Sherlock eagerly walked toward Huldra; even in this dim light, he could see that she was every bit as gorgeous in the slight dark as she was in the light.

As Sherlock approached the end of the bed where Huldra stood, he could look right into her emerald-green eyes. Her lips pouted in a sexy way. She wrapped her arms around Sherlock's neck, caressing the back of his head as they stared into each other's eyes.

"Before we get down to the good part. I was wondering something detective."

Huldra leaned over and bit the bottom of Sherlock's lip. Her bite into his flesh turned him on. It was the type of teasing power that only a woman can wield against him. She released his lip.

"Yes, dear Huldra?"

"Why are you traveling with a Death Dealer?"

Sherlock was confused; surely she meant Carmina. Though the term "Death Dealer" was not one he was familiar with.

He wrapped his arms around her waist, resting his hands on her ass. Her ass distracted him; it bubbled out in just the right way. He couldn't help but think about how good it would feel bouncing on his cock.

"What is a Death Dealer?"

Huldra licked Sherlock's chin with her soft tongue.

"Don't play dumb with me, detective, your travel companion is not what she seems, you and I both know it."

Sherlock kissed Huldra, moving his hand down and squeezing her ass cheek. He slipped his tongue into her mouth until both were wrestling with their saliva back and forth. Until Huldra pulled back from Sherlock, she was proceeding with caution, slowly disarming him.

"Carmina is just a librarian; she is giving me a ride to my next case in Point Pleasant, West Virginia."

Huldra began undoing the knot on Sherlock's necktie in a slow, seductive way.

"Come now, Sherlock, Carmina is the daughter of a powerful witch; she is a Death Dealer. So, either you have a potent ally or a dangerously close enemy. Which one is it?"

Huldra untied Sherlock's tie, and it slid down around his neck until she was holding it in her hand. She proceeded to use the necktie as a blindfold around Sherlock's eyes.

"Carmina is an ally, I assure you. She has done nothing but assist me since I arrived in the States."

Huldra unbuttoned Sherlock's vest, and he slid it down over his shoulders, tossing it on the floor. Next was his white button-down shirt, which Huldra had already begun to unbutton. She finished releasing the long-sleeved shirt, Sherlock untucked it from his pants, took off his shirt, and tossed it onto the motel floor.

"Get on your knees, Sherlock."

Still unable to see through the blindfold, Sherlock carefully lowered to his knees, allowing his hands to slide down Huldra's ass until he felt her ankles. He held one in each hand while she stayed standing on the motel bed.

"I am going to educate you, Sherlock, but on one condition."

He leaned over and kissed her feet.

"What is the condition, Huldra?"

"You take me with you."

This took Sherlock out of the moment; he stopped kissing her feet, tilting his head to one side as if curious as to why she would want to leave with a stranger. Although she was well on her way to fucking him, or so it would seem.

"Take you with me to Point Pleasant? Why?"

As Sherlock was going to say more, Huldra slipped her left foot into his mouth to gag him and shut him up while she spoke. Her toes now resting on his tongue.

"My brother never allows me to leave this desolate place. I can be of use to you on your journey. There seems to be a lot you do not know."

She slipped her foot out of his mouth.

"Huldra, you may not know this, but my cases are dangerous. I hunt monsters, the kind that nightmares are made of."

Sherlock could not see Huldra, but he could hear her; she was undressing. The sound that her bra made when it hit the lampshade gave the detective the promise that he would be able to see her naked body soon.

"Sherlock, stand up slowly."

He complied with Huldra's order.

Once he stood, Huldra got down from the bed.

She stood in front of Sherlock, the top of her head reaching his waist. She began unbuckling his pants.

"I know more about monsters than you do, like the Death Dealer you are with."

Huldra slid off Sherlock's brown leather belt, dropping it on the floor next to him. He placed his hand on her head, assuming that was the moment she would suck his cock... he was wrong.

"No, no, you eat my pussy first."

Sherlock removed his hand from her head. He got down on his knees once again. She sat on the bed and lay back, resting both legs on his shoulders, one on each side. She grabbed a lock of his hair with her hand and pulled his face closer to her pussy lips.

"She is no monster, Huldra."

Sherlock stated as his voice faded away with his lips brushing the hair on her pussy. He couldn't see, but he could feel. Being blindfolded made him more obsessed with eating her pussy.

"Start licking, I will tell you what you need to know."

Sherlock gently bit the lips of Huldra's pussy, first one side and then the other. He positioned his arms under and over her thighs so he could get a solid grasp on her legs, pulling her pussy closer to him. She let out a soft moan.

He began licking her clit slowly, he took long, slow strokes, allowing her pussy to get wet as he squeezed her thighs tighter.

In between moans and rolling her eyes back, she attempted to explain to Sherlock what he clearly did not know.

"Eat my pussy good detective."

She said out loud as he obeyed.

"A Death Dealer is…." She lost her train of thought as he spread her lips open with his tongue, moving it side to side in her.

"A Death Dealer trades souls for cryptids. Oh! fuck that feels good."

The word "cryptid" caught Sherlock's attention. He couldn't stop, though. She was flowing into his mouth, her soft pussy making every bit of her quiver. She could feel the goosebumps on her legs, how they slowly raised the small, almost invisible hairs she had not shaved.

He moved his lips away just enough to speak, then he filled his mouth with her pussy.

"Tell me more."

"Death Dealers trade the souls of humans to cryptids. It allows the monsters to live longer, in some cases changing their forms."

Sherlock moved his right hand away from under Huldra's thigh and slowly moved it up her stomach to her chest until he could feel her breasts. They didn't feel big in his hand, which he didn't mind. He felt for her nipple; the coned shape he could feel of her nipple made his cock throb.

"Fuck yes, eat that pussy!"

She moaned, moving her head from side to side.

Sherlock began kissing her thigh.

"I want to fuck you bad."

The British accent made Huldra even wetter.

"No. Keep eating pussy."

She said as she attempted to catch her breath. Sherlock smiled, moved his face right back into her warm, wet pussy. He kissed her clit, then he gently bit her clit. She could not contain herself, screaming in joy. No one ever bit her clit before; it was a move Sherlock was known to use from time to time.

"Oh my God, now lick it some more."

Sherlock did just that. He bit her clit gently and then licked it in long strokes. Bit it again, followed by more licks.

Huldra huffed. In between breaths, she told Sherlock more. This was her chance to let Sherlock know that she was more than just a good fuck, she had a world of knowledge about monsters and cryptids.

"Le Lechuza protects the monsters, the cryptids... right there keep licking deep."

Sherlock licked down her pussy, all the way to her taint. He placed his hands under her ass and slightly lifted her, allowing him to lick her all the way down to her asshole.

"Yes, baby, that's it, eat my ass good."

Her body was lifted, moving so Sherlock's tongue could lick her asshole just in the right spot.

"The cryptids aren't bad... fuck yes, eat that ass!"

"Cryptids can be killers; some are horrible, but not all are bad."

"Fuck yes, I'm going to cum!"

As Sherlock was eating Huldra's ass, he reached one hand over her, beginning to run his finger over her clit slowly.

"Oh damn!"

She screamed, appreciating that she never climaxed while someone ate her ass before.

Huldra's body shivered for what seemed like minutes but was only several seconds.

"Time for me to fuck you, detective."

Sherlock stood, a bit weak in the legs from kneeling on the cheap motel carpet for a while. He stood up and took off the necktie covering his eyes. He stared at Huldra, appreciating her beauty. Her perfectly coned nipples, her short chunky thighs. He liked it all.

Sherlock pulled down his gray slacks, kicked off his shoes, and pulled down his flannel boxers.

Huldra, still having not recovered her breath fully from her orgasm, moved to her side and stood up again on the bed.

Sherlock crawled onto the bed and lay down, looking up at Huldra.

She straddled one leg over him and squatted down, using her hand to adjust his cock to slide into her.

"I thought you were going to suck my cock first, though I am not complaining."

She placed her hands on his chest, and she started bouncing slowly on his cock.

"Shut the fuck up, Sherlock."

She slid her pussy up and down on him. He grabbed her ankles again, squeezing to hold her in place while she bounced faster on him.

"How does that pussy feel on your cock, detective?"

Last time Sherlock had sex, he could only recall parts of it. So, he was enthusiastic about being fully aware and in the moment. She felt sensational to him; he could not get enough of her.

He could feel the head of his circumcised cock going deep into her. Sherlock prided himself on his sexual ability. He knew he did not have the cock the size of Skookum (Bigfoot), but seven and a half inches never got him any complaints.

"You feel amazing, just keep doing what you are doing."

As she continued riding his cock and working her pussy on him, he slapped her ass. The sound was a loud smack; in part, he thought it might have been too rough.

"Is that all you got, you British fuck? Spank me harder!"

Sherlock slapped her ass again, this time harder, as Huldra requested, which made her moan.

"There we go, Sherlock, that's what I want."

Sherlock knew he wasn't in control; Huldra was. He was completely okay with that.

After several hard pumps, Huldra turned around, riding Sherlock in reverse cowgirl position. She leaned down against his legs, allowing her to work her pussy up and down on him.

The view that Sherlock was looking at was her pussy sliding on him, with the asshole he licked a few moments ago joining in on the bounce.

"Huldra, I'm cumming."

Huldra turned her head to one side to look back at Sherlock.

"Then cum."

She pushed her pussy far deep down his cock, and he came inside of her. She could feel his cock pulsating inside as he filled her with his seed.

"Fuck yes, Huldra!"

Huldra bounced a few more times on his cock for good measure to ensure all his semen was planted deep into her.

She got off him, then lay down next to him, while placing her head on his chest.

"So, Sherlock… What time are we leaving tomorrow?"

Sherlock dropped his head back on the pillow and closed his eyes.

"9 a.m."

He replied with whatever energy he had left.

Chapter 24

The next morning, after Laney fed Bubba Chance to Mothman, she felt refreshed. Whether that is because she was pleasured in the woods by her slave monster or because she was happy that the scumbag who sexually harassed her was dead, she wasn't sure. Though it seemed it was a combination of both. Just as she began her day, her aunt called for her from downstairs.

"Laney, come down here right away."

Laney put her robe on, making her way down the staircase. The staircase ended a few feet from the front door. Standing at the doorway were two uniformed police officers.

"Laney, these officers have some questions about your boss, Bubba Chance."

Laney knew this would inevitably happen; after all, several of her coworkers saw her leave with Bubba.

The first mustachioed officer stepped forward.

"Hi Laney, I am Officer Owens. We found Bubba Chance's car off the highway. Though we hadn't found him yet, there was a substantial amount of blood at the scene. Your coworkers told us you left with him yesterday. Is that correct?"

The best way to tell a lie is always to infuse a bit of truth into it. It makes it more believable, more deliberate.

"Yes, he gave me a ride home after my aunt's car wouldn't start."

She was able to morph her face to show genuine concern, though her soul was grinning inside.

"What time would you say he dropped you off? We are trying to get a timeline of when this accident may have happened to him."

The officer didn't seem to be much of an investigator, something Laney could use to her advantage.

"Well, I am not sure. He mentioned something when he dropped me off about needing a drink after a long day."

Bubba Chance would often visit the local watering hole; it was known around town that he enjoyed a good drink.

"I see, well, thank you for your time. If you could think of anything else that would be useful to us, don't hesitate to get in touch with the station."

"Absolutely, I hope Bubba is okay."

Laney's voice was sincere, too bad for the police; it was utter bullshit. She felt no remorse for feeding her asshole boss to her Mothman.

With that, the police officers left. Laney's aunt stared at her niece.

"Laney, what is going on? You have been acting strangely, and now someone is missing, someone who you were the last to see."

Laney did not like lying to her aunt, but would her aunt believe her if she told the truth? Probably not.

"Tia, Bubba gave me a ride home yesterday. I don't know what happened after that."

Her aunt knew there was more, so she did something she didn't often do. She invoked the name of Laney's mother, who is no longer around.

"You know if my sister Selma were here, you would tell her the truth!"

It stung Laney, but the verbal assault wasn't enough for her to come clean.

"My mother is gone; she could be dead or living another life. I do not live my life worried about what my mother would think. She lost that right when she left."

"There is still much you do not understand about your mother. She would want you to be safe. I need to know you are safe."

Laney walked over to her aunt. She grabbed her hands in her own, looking her aunt in the eyes.

"I promise you, Tia, I am as safe as I have ever been."

Something about that statement made her aunt feel reassured and scared at the same time.

"I need to get ready for class."

"How do you intend on getting there?"

"I will call Jordie."

With that, Laney went back upstairs. Laney's aunt walked over to the telephone, picked up the receiver, dialed the required numbers, and waited for an answer.

Until finally, there was a response on the other line.

"Yes, it's Monica. I think my niece has had an encounter with one of our associates."

Chapter 25

Carmina, driving her vehicle, was in hyper annoyance mode. For her life, could she understand why they picked up Huldra as a passenger, she knew that must have been Sherlock's date the prior night.

"Tell me again why this person is traveling with us?"

Carmina remained silent during the car ride but could not hide her contempt.

"Huldra is very skilled in…."

Huldra smiled from the back seat as Carmina rolled her eyes.

"She is skilled in the knowledge of the world of cryptids. We could use her expertise on this. Also, she is an adult, she asked to come with us, and I agreed."

Sherlock's voice had a matter-of-fact tone.

"Just make sure she doesn't get in your way, Sherlock. If you like, I could keep an eye on her."

Carmina spoke as if Huldra weren't in the vehicle.

"I will be of use to Sherlock; I know lots about the underworld he is embarking on. Maybe not as much as you, but I could be of use."

Huldra sounded confident, assured of herself in this instance.

"We will be in Point Pleasant soon enough, Sherlock. This woman is your responsibility."

"I can take care of myself, Carmina. I do not need Sherlock to do it."

"I'm going to take a nap while you two ladies verbally spar. Please wake me when we get there."

Sherlock slid down in the passenger seat and tilted his deerstalker hat forward to cover his eyes. After several minutes of silence, Sherlock began to snore.

Carmina looked in the rearview mirror, glaring at Huldra as she looked back at the driver.

"Why did you want to come along with him?"

Carmina's voice was accusatory.

"Because he eats a mean pussy."

Huldra's reply made her smile, thinking of the night before.

"I know what you are, Carmina. Not every day I get to meet a Death Dealer; your kind is the stuff of legend."

Carmina gripped the steering wheel as hard as she could, her white knuckles becoming apparent to the naked eye.

"Careful, Huldra, get in my way and I will feed your soul to a Wendigo."

This made Huldra very nervous; she knew Carmina had influence in the dark world, and Huldra didn't take her threat lightly.

"Do not worry, Carmina, I have no intention of crossing you. For the record, I needed to escape my brother's reign over me, plus Sherlock is a good lay."

Carmina said nothing else as she continued her drive down the highway.

Chapter 26

Laney was at her college campus, exiting the building where her humanities class was located. Jordie gave her a lift to campus. News of Bubba Chance's disappearance quickly spread throughout Point Pleasant. The restaurant would be closed until further notice so that no work would take place tonight.

As she walked across the courtyard, she could see the jerk Brian East with his goon friends. One of his friends broke away from the group and approached Laney, which made her stop in her tracks.

"Hey, sweet girl, hold on for a moment."

Laney looked at the douche bag jock standing in front of her. He would be considered moderately attractive by most women. However, Laney didn't pay much attention to his looks. He didn't have wings, and as she figured out lately, wings are a turn-on for her.

"Look, my friend, Brian over there said that you give an amazing blowjob. I was wondering if I could take you out tonight to the woods so you can give me one too."

Laney looked over and could see Brian with his jackal friends staring at them, all while laughing out loud.

She was pissed; she didn't know what to say or do. Her eyes got watery from embarrassment. Brian, being the complete prick he was, told his buddy that Laney was easy to score with, lying about Laney going down on him.

"What do you say, Laney? Brian says big girls suck the best cock."

The jock adorned a smug arrogance on his face, putting on a show for his mates.

"What's your name?"

Laney asked in a broken voice.

"I'm Matt."

Laney wrote something on a piece of notebook paper, tore the page, and handed it to Matt the goon.

"Here is my address, pick me up this afternoon at 4: 00 p.m."

"You got it."

Matt walked away back towards his group of moronic friends, lifting the piece of paper with her address in the air as if to show a conquered land he had just invaded.

Laney walked away. Once the embarrassment subsided, a sinister smile returned to her face.

****

Matt pulled up his mint green 1952 Pontiac Chieftain. The car was several years old but was still in great shape. Laney stepped out of her aunt's house wearing a black dress with slits up her thighs on each side. The dress exposed her back, sporting a gothic look. Her eyeliner was black, making her purple eye shadow look vibrant.

As she approached the vehicle, she saw Matt in the driver's seat and two other guys in the back of the car.

Laney was hesitant to get into the car. Matt had the passenger window rolled down.

"Are you going to get in or what?"

"Who are those guys in the back of the car?"

Laney knew she would be outnumbered.

"Get in, then I'll tell you."

She could see Matt and the other two passengers laughing.

Laney opened the car door, sat inside, and slammed the door shut.

Matt sped off fast from in front of Laney's house.

"This is Jerry in the white sweater; that's Kirk in the back corner."

Matt kept the introduction brief.

"Why are they in the car? I thought we were going on a ...date."

Laney knew her fears would be coming true as soon as Matt spoke.

"Well, see it's like this, me and the fellas figured why keep all that good mouth just to myself. So, I figured you wouldn't mind sucking off my friends also, slut."

The idiots in the back seat laughed out loud; they found it funny how he spoke down to her.

Laney's insides were crawling, angry with a not-so-healthy dose of fear.

She turned around to look at the guys sitting behind her, then back at Matt.

"I know a good spot we could go to."

She had a spot she knew well, a place where she could be her true, dominating self.

The guys in the back of the car hooted and hollered at the prospect of getting their cocks sucked tonight. Matt smiled.

"I told you guys Brian was right, she is a slut."

Matt said out loud as he kept speeding down the street and onto the highway.

Laney said nothing; she stared forward in silence while the guys in the back cracked open cans of beer. As the pines got closer, the small town disappeared off the highway.

She directed Matt to the exit off the highway.

"Is this the same spot you fucked Brian?"

Kirk's voice was filled with disrespect.

"Actually, yes, it is."

Laney was going to play into this role of being easy to screw. For the moment, anyway.

"Man, this girl is wild!"

Jerry was so excited and drunk that he couldn't contain his eagerness.

Matt pulled into the same grass opening in the woods that Bubba Chance had met his deadly, albeit deserved fate.

Matt put the car in park and turned it off.

"Well, I'm going first because I drove."

He began to unbuckle his belt, but Laney stopped him.

"Not here, behind that tree."

Before Matt could protest, Laney had the car door open, she had stepped out, and began walking into the woods. She walked to the front of the grassy opening, beckoning him with her finger.

Matt left the car in haste, and he followed Laney to the woods, behind a thick tree.

She grabbed Matt and pushed him against the tree trunk.

Laney stepped back a few feet, staring at Matt.

Matt unbuckled his belt, took off his pants, then pulled out his cock.

Laney laughed. She couldn't help it; it was as if all the jocks were in the same small dick club.

"What the fuck are you laughing at Bitch?"

Matt was upset and embarrassed, with a slight mix of humiliation.

"I'm laughing at you. You walk around with your friends like you're some big shots. You treat women like shit, and you have the nerve to do all this with a dick that small."

This is how Laney's darker side took over with confidence, strength, and malice.

"Fuck you, get over here, suck my dick like you said you would."

"Mothy, time to come out and play."

Laney's words were stone cold, a direct demand to see her monster. Mothman did not disappoint.

With a large thud landing behind Laney, the Mothman stood up and expanded his wings behind her. He looked terrifying, with bright red eyes, a heavy chain around its neck, and wings that looked as if gargoyles had made them.

"What the fuck?!"

Matt's small penis attempted to shrivel and retreat inside him.

"This is Mothman, he's my Mothman. He's my lover."

"That fucking monster is your lover. I'm getting the fuck out of here."

The dumb jock attempted to pull up his jeans until Laney gave a command to Vlad.

"Vlad, my love, eat his heart for me."

No sooner had she said that than Mothman flew towards Matt, pushing his torso against the tree.

Mothman stared his glowing red eyes at Matt, trancing him. He clawed into Matt's chest as blood began to spurt out of his chest.

Matt was still alive enough to feel Mothman's claws scraping into his chest cavity, shattering bones until he reached his heart. The Mothman ripped out the bloody, still beating heart. Matt's body collapsed to the ground.

Mothman then clenched his fangs around the pumping heart, drinking the blood dry.

"Good boy, Vlad, very good."

Vlad walked towards his master, blood dripping from his lips.

Laney grabbed the chain around Mothman's neck, pulling it closer to her.

"Now, slave, time for you to please your master."

"Yes, my queen."

Laney walked to the tree trunk, stepping over Matt's carcass.

"I want you to fuck me, over his dead body."

Vlad walked toward Laney. She put her arms on his slick shoulders.

Mothman grabbed her by her hips, lifting her so she could wrap her thick legs around him.

He pushed her against the tree trunk. Her dress was falling on both sides of her legs.

She kissed his lips, licking Vlad's fangs.

He pushed his forked tongue out into her mouth, caressing it.

Mothman's two-headed cock began to emerge; she could feel it touching her pussy. She was glad she had the foresight not to wear panties tonight.

He began licking her neck, and she rotated her head in relaxation. She was enjoying her monster.

Mothman's fangs extended out, and he sank them into Laney's neck. She pulled the feathered fur from behind his neck. He began sucking her blood softly, the blood flowing out of her and into him felt euphoric to her.

Her pussy moistened, and she could feel his first cock head slowly go into her. It stretched her wide, while he continued to suck on her neck.

Mothman inserted his second cock head into her; that was the fit she wanted. The one that filled her.

****

"My mistress feels so good on my cock. Her blood, just like her juices, strengthens me, invigorates my life force."

Laney moaned as Mothman released her neck; his tongue then began licking her chest down to her breast that was still tucked into her dress.

"The body of this idiot I killed, I can feel his bones crunching under my talons."

Mothman slowly moved one cock head out of her pussy, slowly sliding it into her ass. His cock head was so wet from her, it served as a natural lubricant to allow him inside of her in both holes.

Laney moved her arms from around Vlad's shoulders, instead opting to grab the thick chain she placed around his neck. She held it tight as he entered both of her holes at the same time. Though the cock in her pussy felt great, the one in her ass would take a little getting used to. Although the forbidden desire arouses her.

The magnetic force that Mothman felt in his chest connecting him to his master was pulsating. He was so deep in her, it felt as if they were one.

He continued to bite her neck, taking in just droplets of her blood into his fangs.

With every thrust, her body would bump up against the tree trunk behind her.

"Go slow, my slave."

Mothman obliged, slowly taking out both cocks, then sliding them back in with ease. Allowing them both to appreciate every inch that was going into her.

The forest around them swirled into a blur. Laney pulled the chain around Vlad's neck so he could continue to thrust into her pussy and ass. Both of her holes were welcoming him with moist delight.

When Vlad released her neck, Laney did something unexpected.

She bit Mothman on his neck; she could feel his skin, his small feathers in her mouth.

Biting down hard, drawing some of his blood into her mouth. Vlad moaned in excitement, his passion for her further ignited. He began fucking her harder, the deeper she bit him, the harder he fucked her.

"That bite she has, it makes me weak. I will continue to thrust her harder with every inch she bites down with."

Mothman fluttered his wings as they fucked. When Laney looked down, she noticed they were five feet off the ground. She could feel the trunk of the tree rub against her back as she slid up. Her legs wrapped around his waist allowed her to have an iron grip. Her body was not going to let him go.

Vlad's wings fluttered in the air as he continued to embrace her body with his two-headed cock.

She stopped biting him to stare into his glowing red eyes. The beams of light from his eyes cast her face in a red glow.

"I need your juice, my queen. Please allow me to drink from you."

Laney knew what juice the Mothman truly wanted; it wasn't her blood.

"Keep fucking me, Mothy. I will let you know when your mistress is ready for you to drink her."

She was empowered, confident, and enjoying every moment of her monster fucking both of her holes.

"Yes, my master."

He was obedient, only to her. That power over him emboldened her; the mere thought made her wet.

She could feel his girthy cock sliding into both of her holes, her ass feeling more comfortable with his cock in it.

Her asshole contracted around his cock, her pussy feeling every vein in his cock vibrating inside of her. Every in and out motion from Vlad would slightly rub his groin feathers against her clit, continuously stimulating her.

"She's getting close to giving me her nectar, I can feel it getting close, building within her thighs as they wrap me around her tighter."

Laney tilted her head back, letting out a soothing moan. The stimulation from both holes was bringing her closer to climaxing.

Laney's body began to shiver. This orgasm began to feel different; it encompassed all of her. As the goosebumps crawled over her skin, Mothman's wings expanded again a bit further, pushing his cock into her again with a final thrust.

"Your nectar is about to be ready, my slave."

Mothman gently glided them back down to the ground base of the tree, while still inside of her.

"Now, my love, to your knees."

Mothman slid his cocks out of her, kneeling in front of her. She placed one leg over his shoulder. He took out his forked tongue, beginning to lick her clit as she was quaking from her intense orgasm.

"I'm cumming, Mothy!"

As soon as the words came out of her mouth, so did her juices; she sprayed right into Mothman's tongue. She could feel his soft forked tongue licking the inside of her vaginal walls.

"Yes! Drink it, slave, drink all of it!"

Laney placed her right hand on Vlad's head and grasped hard at his feathered hair.

Vlad drank every drop of her gushingness.

Once she was satisfied he got it all, she released his head from her grip.

"That's a good monster."

Mothman placed his claw-like hand around her waist, resting his head on her stomach.

Laney stroked his head while staring at the corpse that was under them.

"Our work isn't done yet, my love. There are two others back in the car we must deal with."

"Allow me, my queen. I will dispose of them."

"Very well, come back here once you finish."

Mothman flew straight up in the air, disappearing among the treetops.

The two guys, Kirk and Jerry, were outside Matt's car drinking beer. They hadn't realized how long they had been there since they were halfway drunk.

"What do you think is taking them so long?"

Jerry asked, eager for his turn at Laney.

"Who knows, she probably wanted him to fuck her too."

They both laughed until some movement in the trees above stopped their laughter.

Jerry looked up to see two red glowing eyes in the trees above.

"What the fuck is that?"

He pointed to the tree above them to help Kirk see what he was seeing.

Suddenly, the eyes they were seeing became larger. The winged beast dropped in front of two drunken frat boys.

They were both petrified by the monster they were looking at. Mothman grinned his blood-soaked fangs at them for good measure.

"It's a fucking monster!"

Kirk screamed as he threw his beer can at Mothman, bouncing off its chest.

Mothman looked down at where the beer can hit him with slight amusement.

Jerry ran towards the car, diving into the passenger side window, sliding in franticness into the driver's seat. He turned on the car, much to Kirk's surprise.

Mothman flew towards Kirk, grabbed his body midair as he attempted to run away, and took him above the car.

As Jerry dropped the shift into reverse, he began backing up at an incredible pace. Then a loud sound hit the top of the car.

BLAM!

The sound made him slam on the brakes, which allowed the bloody body of Kirk to roll off the roof of the car and onto the front windshield.

Jerry screamed in horror to see his friend, now a bloody mess on the car hood. The impact of being dropped from a high altitude is entirely on display.

The panicked driver continued his course in reverse.

Vlad was going to chase him until Laney came out from behind the tree.

"Let him go, him being drunk, no one will believe what he says. Then he will have to answer as to what happened to his two friends."

A wolf appeared out of the tree line, though it caught Laney by surprise, she was not scared. Truthfully, she didn't even flinch.

"My queen, may we give what is left of the carcasses to this wolf?"

"Yes, you may."

Mothman nodded at the wolf, who then went and dragged the lifeless body of Kirk into the woods.

"Come, my slave, back to your tree. Time for your queen and you to do some monster cuddling."

Chapter 27

Watson sat in his new motel room staring at the plague doctor mask. What started as an attempt to find out information about a secret society has turned into murder. The phone rang in his room; he was right next to it. He allowed it to ring three more times before answering the call.

"Hello?"

"Dr. Watson, I was told you needed to speak with me?"

It was Carmen on the line, the woman or witch who orchestrated him becoming a murderer. He was going to despise her for it.

"Carmen, I did as you asked. Ripshaw is gone."

"I'm aware, Watson, you did well. Is that what you wanted to tell me?"

"I don't want to be a part of this anymore. You can keep your secret society and all the bullshit it comes with. I am out; do you understand me?"

His voice was firm, the tone of a man who was at his wits' end with his internal struggles.

"Well, I am indeed sorry you feel that way, Watson. I mean, this was your task to be part of La Lechuza. It seems like a waste to go through all that trouble for nothing."

"What do you mean?"

"You performed a task, a task to eliminate a rogue ex-member of our organization. With that elimination, you may take his place. In our circle, you will be known as the Plague Doctor."

Watson thought for a moment about how many more of these horrible deeds would be a part of the organization's yield.

"Carmen, I killed a man in cold blood."

"Wrong, you killed a murderer. There is a distinction. Ripshaw hurt many people, including a beloved member of our organization."

"Yes, but why did it have to be me?"

Watson, still grasping for answers, sounded desperate.

"You came to me, Watson, don't forget that. I did you a favor, first letting you live, then allowing you to be a part of something bigger than you, something greater than you."

"So, what, I am supposed to live my life as your errand boy? Killing people at your every whim?"

Carmen sounded exasperated.

"Here is the deal, Watson, you have the mask of the Plague Doctor. Tell me, did you wear it?"

The silence on the phone line was deafening. Watson did not reply to her.

"I will take your silence as meaning you did adorn the mask. Did you enjoy it?"

Watson thought for a moment of flashbacks of torturing Ripshaw for answers; the truth was, he did enjoy it, he relished every moment of it.

"Yes, alright, yes, I did enjoy it. What does that have anything to do with it?"

"Watson, when you came to my library that day in London, digging for information about my coven, I knew something about you was different. The mask picks the person, not the other way around. Had you worn that mask and felt nothing, then the offer would not have been intended for you."

More silence from Dr. John Watson as he stared at the mask.

"He killed many people, innocent people. He poisoned their water supplies, children, and the elderly. I am not that man."

"Of course you aren't, Watson. I know the deed you did was not pleasant, but it was necessary. I promise you will never be asked to take the life of an innocent person or being. You can change the narrative about our organization's Plague Doctor. This is me asking you to take a natural place in our society."

"I am not that kind of doctor, Carmen."

"You are now Watson."

"Take the mask, stay in the states for a while, when you are ready, return to London as the Plague Doctor."

"If I choose not to?"

"We both know that isn't an option, John."

Carmen hung up the phone.

Watson placed the receiver down, and almost immediately, he heard a knock on his motel door.

When he opened the door, there was a red box on the mat outside his motel room. He reached down and grabbed the box, bringing it inside his room.

Upon opening the box, a gold pin sat on a black cushion. The pin was the body of an owl, with the face of a woman. It was the symbol of La Lechuza.

Chapter 28

Sherlock, Carmina, Huldra, and Thor just passed the sign that read "*Welcome to Point Pleasant.*"

The journey did not seem as long as the one to Roanoke. Sherlock was eager to get to work; cryptids intrigued him. Thor was nestled in the back seat with Huldra, saving his energy for when he would have to spring into action.

As they entered town, three police cars with their sirens blaring drove past them.

"Where do you think they are going?"

Sherlock asked with intrigue.

"I'm not sure, but we should go to the police station first to gather whatever reports we can about the winged monster people are claiming to see."

Sherlock agreed, while Huldra stayed quiet.

Carmina seemed to know the town very well. Sherlock took mental note that she did not have to ask for directions; the roads were clearly second nature to her.

"You seem to know your way around this town pretty well, Carmina."

His voice sounded suspicious of her.

"I have been here before; do not worry, I have a contact in the police department who may be able to help us."

Carmina pulled up to the red-brick police station.

"Shall we take our exit?"

Huldra asked with delight.

"We sound like too many people; Sherlock and I will go. You stay in the car."

"She comes with us, Carmina. We need her assistance."

Sherlock was defiant, but his defense of Huldra was enough for her to carry a smug smile as all three of them exited the vehicle. Carmina did not push back against Sherlock's request for Huldra to join them inside the station. Thor stayed in the car.

The three of them entered the station. It seemed like a bustling place on this day. Uniformed police officers were moving around frantically. Carmina approached the front desk and asked for Officer Owens.

The receptionist walked to the back office, and within a few moments, Officer Owens appeared at the front desk.

"Carmina, what a surprise."

"Owens, it's been a while. This is my friend Sherlock and his girlfriend, I guess."

"Don't be petty, Carmina."

Sherlock said while reaching his arm out to shake Officer Owen's hand.

"What could I help you with?"

It appeared to Sherlock that the mere presence of Carmina obliged the officer to help them; in his experience, this was not the norm.

"I am investigating the case of your winged creature, the man who looks like a moth."

"Ah, yes, there has been a lot of interest about that around here. It's just some drunks thinking they saw things in the sky."

Officer Owens seemed a bit dismissive of any real danger.

"As a matter of fact, we got some college kid in here now claiming some monster killed his friends in the woods. We dispatched some officers out there to see if they could locate his missing classmates."

"How many people have been reported missing in the past month?"

The officer sighed and looked over his shoulder to ensure everyone else in the station was busy and not eavesdropping on their conversation.

"Well, lately there have been a few things to strike this town hard. First, some campers went missing, then a hiker. A local restaurant owner had a car accident right off the highway. We haven't located his body yet, but we fear the worst. Now we have two college kids missing in the woods. All while people are claiming to see a monster."

"That seems like a lot of mystery for a small town like Point Pleasant."

Sherlock knew that these circumstances were more than mere coincidence.

"May I speak to the young man who saw the monster?"

"No can-do, mister. This is police business; I wouldn't even be able to bring you back into the interrogation room without raising alarms and suspicion here. Maybe it's best if we handle it."

"Owens, we will return to the car. In approximately five minutes, the vehicle will be behind the police station. Bring out the witness, allow Sherlock to question him, then he will return inside."

Officer Owens seemed to take Carmina's exact order, as if he worked for her. Sherlock couldn't help but notice that the officer wore a watch; on the face of the watch was an owl with a woman's face—a symbol he had seen several times before.

"Five minutes, we do not have much time. I'll meet you in the back."

The team of three returned to the car, Carmina started the engine, and quickly drove around the back of the building.

After a moment, Officer Owens appeared from the backdoor entrance to the station. The nervous witness was next to him.

"Why am I out here? You guys should be in the woods looking for that monster that killed my friend!"

Jerry's voice is on edge.

"Calm down, son, this man here investigates these types of occurrences. His name is Sherlock. Tell him what you told me."

Sherlock exited the car. He walked up to Jerry and greeted him with a warm smile.

"Good day, young man. My name is Sherlock Holmes, and I am investigating a series of strange occurrences in Point Pleasant. I am very intrigued by what happened to you."

"So, you believe me? You believe there is a monster in the woods?"

Jerry was longing for approval from anyone who would believe him.

"Of course I do. I am certain you saw something. Please tell what happened."

Sherlock attempted to comfort the witness.

"Well, Kirk, Matt, and I went out to the woods to have some beers. We were hanging out, having a good time. Then this monster came out of nowhere, and he slashed at me, but I managed to push him off. Matt ran into the woods, and the monster grabbed Kirk. The winged creature hypnotized Kirk, slashing his throat, then it flew away."

"What complete bullshit."

Huldra said as everyone turned to her.

"He's lying!"

Huldra exclaimed.

Sherlock turned back to face Jerry.

"Indeed, he is my dear. At no point have you told me how you were able to escape."

Officer Owens glanced at Jerry, lifting one eyebrow, hoping sincerely that this frat boy didn't waste his time.

"Well, I…"

Jerry had no answer; he hadn't figured out that part of his lie yet.

Sherlock took a step closer to Jerry, looking very annoyed.

"I can help you, only if you tell me the truth. Almost the entire time you were speaking to me, your eyes were fixated on looking down and towards the left. That is a tall tale sign of someone fabricating something in their mind. Somehow in this story, you were heroic enough to take a swipe at the monster, but not heroic enough to help your friends. As Huldra stated, your story thus far, young man, is bullshit."

"Hey, man, I was reporting a crime. I know what I saw."

Jerry was defensive that the detective so easily deconstructed his lie.

"Were you with anyone else who could corroborate your story?"

The detective knew there was more to the story.

"Just some girl from campus."

Jerry muttered under his breath.

Officer Owens was annoyed. Jerry never mentioned anyone other than the three of them.

"Why would a lady want to be alone in the woods with three college guys?"

Huldra asked in a sarcastic tone.

"Very funny, Huldra," Carmina said flatly.

"Okay, so Matt asked this girl out to go to the woods for some fun time. She was so eager, like we were told, that Kirk and I joined them because we figured she would be generous with all of us."

"You fucking piece of shit!"

Carmina was getting angry at this failed frat boy.

"Who told you?"

Sherlock questioned Jerry; all eyes were on him now.

"What?"

"Who told you she was eager?"

Sherlock's tone turned serious. What if the person who told them that she was eager staged the whole thing?

"My friend Brian East went to the woods a couple of weeks ago, I think. He said she begged him for sex, so he felt sorry for her, and they had sex."

"So, where is this girl now? She could surely tell us if she saw a monster."

He was getting to the bottom of something, though he wasn't quite sure what it was yet.

"I don't know, she went into the woods, I never saw her after that. Her name is Laney, and she goes to our campus. She works at Chance's Burgers."

"What did the monster look like?"

Sherlock was getting to that question, but Carmina beat him to it.

"Red glowing eyes, large wings, razor sharp fangs, a fucking nightmare is what it looked like."

That might have been the sincerest thing that Jerry has stated throughout the entire conversation.

"Thank you, Officer Owens, Jerry, for your time."

The witness walked back into the station, and Carmina, Sherlock, and Huldra shuffled back into the vehicle.

"Where are we going now?"

Huldra asked with curiosity.

"We are going to Chance's Burgers so I can find this girl and ask her questions about what she saw last night. I assume Carmina already knows the way."

Carmina smiled at Sherlock and nodded as they made their way to Laney's job.

Chapter 29

The trio arrived at Chance's Burgers to find the place had been shuttered. There was only one car in the parking lot.

Sherlock walked to the front counter, which had a roll-down cage indicating it was closed. With a sign attached that read:

"It is with great regret that we must close for the foreseeable future. Our prayers will bring Bubba back to us soon."

"Really wish Officer Owens had mentioned that part."

Carmina looked at Sherlock to guess his next move.

"Let's go to this college campus and see if we can find this Brian East fellow."

"Probably the only lead we have right now."

Huldra and Sherlock exchanged flirtatious smiles.

"Can you two please keep it in your pants? We have work to do."

Carmina was over the two of them making googly eyes at each other.

"Yes, also, I think it would be wise to get a hotel for the night. Two rooms this time."

Sherlock reached down to hold Huldra's hand.

"Okay, get in the fucking car, all of you."

They complied with Carmina's demand and entered the car.

As the car door reopened, Thor began to wake up, annoyed by the commotion.

****

On campus, Laney was walking with pep in her step. The heart was filled with a mix of love, infatuation, and lust. One less douche bag on this Earth, her sexual urges were being satisfied like she had never dreamed of. Laney was happy, of course, but that was quickly interrupted when Brian East came barreling towards her.

"What the fuck did you do to Matt and Kirk?!"

His voice was filled with rage; he already despised Laney, and now it was manic hatred.

"Back off fucko, I didn't do anything to your friends!"

"I know you took them out there to fuck them. You did something to them, I know you did!"

The loud voices drew attention from people walking past on campus.

"Look, I already told you I don't know what happened. They never picked me up."

Brian got close to Laney's face, uncomfortably close.

"You fucking bitch, Matt told me you wanted to fuck him. Jerry saw you going into the woods, so I know you are lying. You won't get away with this."

"Now that is horrible language to use in front of a young lady, sir."

The voice was velvet smooth with a British accent.

Brian turned around to see a man in a wool coat, a brown vest, smoking a cannabis cigarette. Behind him were a younger woman who seemed very angry and a smaller woman with a leash holding a dachshund.

"Who the fuck are you three?"

Brian's voice filled with its regular arrogance.

"I am Sherlock Holmes, detective, world traveler, dog owner, lover."

"Sherlock Holmes? I have heard of you."

Laney said with some dismay. She followed international articles; she was familiar with the cases of Sherlock Holmes and Dr. John Watson.

When Sherlock looked at Laney, something happened. Sherlock felt as if he had met her or seen her somewhere before. The familiarity was one that he could not get over or place.

"Do I know you, Laney?"

Sherlock took a few steps closer to her. He looked into her eyes; that window to the soul seemed like one he had looked through before.

"I have never met you before, Mr. Holmes."

Laney was calm but confused by the presence of these three individuals.

"Get the fuck out of here! I am having a private conversation."

Brian always acted like a bigshot, until he wasn't.

Brian noticed something hitting his feet. When he looked down, Thor had lifted his furry black leg, doused the college boy's foot with urine, then walked back to Huldra, who was holding his leash.

"That fucking dog just pissed on me!"

Sherlock turned towards Brian. He fixed his tie, adjusted his cuffs, dropped his cannabis cigarette, and then grabbed Brian by the throat, catching everyone off guard.

Brian grabbed for Sherlock's arms, but he had a death grip on his neck.

"Apologize to the ladies for using such vulgar language."

The detective's grip squeezed harder, as his stone-cold stare told Brian he meant business.

"I'm sorry."

"Now apologize to Thor."

"Sorry, dog."

Brian was able to cough out; Sherlock then released his hand from around Brian's throat. Brian held his throat, coughing more to recapture some of the air he lost.

"Now, Laney, I do have some questions for you. For you as well, young man."

Brian turned, running away from Sherlock.

"Is there somewhere private we can speak?"

Sherlock asked Laney.

"Yes, we can go to the park across the street. They have picnic tables; no one ever goes there during class time."

Laney felt that drawing the three inquisitive individuals away from campus would create less of a scene.

The four of them walked across the street, as Jordie looked on from a distance.

Once in the park, Sherlock could give himself a proper introduction.

"Thank you for talking with us. As I stated before, my name is Sherlock Holmes, this is Carmina and Huldra. We are investigating a series of sightings of a winged beast. These sightings began to be accompanied by people disappearing."

Laney looked at the three of them, nodding in understanding.

"Were you home last night?"

Laney knew that this was the time to blend honesty with lies. Chances were, by now, Jerry must have told them she was present.

"No, I was not home last night."

"Where were you then?"

Carmina was not great at interrogating; she had the subtlety of a bulldozer.

"I had a date with a friend of that moron who was screaming at me."

Sherlock took over the questioning.

"Was it just the two of you?"

"No, when his friend picked me up, there were two other guys in the backseat. They thought I was easy and that they would get a quick score. At first, I wasn't going to get into the car, but I was worried that they would just keep harassing me if I didn't."

"Thank you, Laney, for your honesty. Could you tell me where you went?"

"We went to a spot in the woods; we had been there before."

"We?"

That slight slip of the tongue was a costly mistake for Laney.

"I meant I have been in that spot before."

In Sherlock's thoughts, that slip meant she was lying at least in part about the things she was saying.

"Then what happened?"

"Matt asked me to go into the woods with him, so I did. Once we started walking, it was so dark that I didn't know if he was still behind me. The next thing I know, I hear screaming and the car screeching in reverse as it left."

"Laney, would you be willing to take us to the woods? To the same spot you were at?"

"Sure, I don't mind. But I must go home now to care for my aunt. Could we go tomorrow?"

"Absolutely, we really appreciate your time."

Laney wrote down her address as she had before and ripped the page out of the notebook. Huldra snatched it from Carmina before she could get the address.

Laney walked away from the park, back across the street toward the campus.

Carmina felt something when Laney was close to her. There was an intense energy radiating from Laney's soul. This meant Laney had some dark gifts, whether she knew it or not.

Chapter 30

That afternoon, when Laney got home, she decided to give her aunt some more information about why three strangers would show up at her house the next day.

She felt bad lying to her aunt about where she had been, about taking her car, about everything.

"Tia, I need to speak with you."

Laney's aunt was in the kitchen, slicing some lemons. She placed the knife down on the counter and walked to the living room, where Laney was sitting on the couch. Since her mother left, Laney has typically told her aunt only the necessary information. The fact that she wanted to have a conversation meant it was something serious.

She sat down, looking at Laney with concern.

"What is it, Laney?"

Laney took a deep breath.

"The other night, I went on a date, kind of."

Her aunt immediately sat up, attentive.

"Laney, did someone hurt you? Did something happen?"

"No, Tia, not really."

"Some guy I went out with told his friends I was easy. Even though I didn't do anything with him, his friend asked me out, and I said yes."

A look of anger began to creep across her aunt Monica's face in anticipation of hearing that some dirtbag tried to get fresh with her.

"When I went out with him, I got into the car, and I noticed there were two other guys there. We went to the pine woods off the highway. I know they wanted to get laid. That is not why I went."

"Why would you get into a car with three college guys, Laney?"

"I meant to, I wanted to feed my monster."

Her aunt instantly went pale; all the blood flushed from her face.

"What monster?"

"The one inside of me, Tia, I have a taste for blood."

"You are no monster, Laney."

"But I am, I have this energy inside of me, I get excited when I see my monster feed. It turns me on, makes me feel powerful. Tia, I'm a monster too."

"What monster are you talking about?"

Laney took another deep breath.

"The one people are claiming to see in the woods. The Mothman is real. I've seen him. I have been with him; I have fed him."

Aunt Monica stood up from her seat, walking over to her wooden cabinet in the living room that housed books. She pulled one book off the shelf, then returned to her seat.

Laney's aunt opened the book, and she produced a photograph of a beautiful, curvy woman with long black hair.

Aunt Monica leaned over, handing the photograph to Laney.

"This is a picture of your mother, Selma. I know you remember her. Your mother is a mighty woman; she lives between two plains, one of the living, another of the dead."

"Tia, what are you saying?"

"Your mother is special; she always had the gift of paranormal magic, but she was cursed long ago. You had a brother, but he died at birth. It was a curse your mother would have to live with for years. She would cry in the night like a banshee at the thought she would never have another child due to the curse. Then you came along, her miracle. To keep you safe, she left you in my charge."

"I had a brother. Where is my mom now?"

There was so much information flooding Laney's thoughts that she began to feel overwhelmed, but she was interested in any information she could find about her mother.

"Your mom is not dead, but she is also not alive. She often passes through the veil of this life and the next."

"What does this have to do with my monster?"

"Laney, I always knew you would have a gift of some sort. This monster, this Mothman, has shown himself to you. Yet you look unharmed, which means you must have some power over him."

Laney thought to herself and smirked, "Hell yes, pussy power."

"That is what I am trying to tell you, Tia, I am his master, he is my slave! I think I love him, but I don't know what that feels like. What I do know is he needed blood to feed, so I brought him some meals. I know, it's fucked up, but I do not even feel bad about it. I lust for my monster; he devours my heart and my enemies."

Her aunt, unafraid of Laney's confession, did her best to make her niece feel as comfortable as possible. She knew this conversation made her vulnerable.

"That is what I am trying to tell you, Lancy, it's in your blood to be part of this world. Whether that's ghosts like your mother or cryptids like your monster."

Laney looked down at the wooden boards under her feet. Was it in her blood to be attracted to a monster? Why was her aunt being so understanding about this?

"You aren't mad at me, Tia?"

"Mad at you? Of course not, if I could get over your mother being La Llorona (Yo-Ro-Na), I can certainly handle you being a monster fucker."

They both laughed out loud.

"Well, Tia, you need to explain to me later what La Llorona is. Right now, we have some people poking their noses around."

Laney explained to her aunt that a visit from the three strangers was scheduled for the following day. She and her aunt devised a plan to keep them as far away as possible from Mothman's trail.

Chapter 31

Sherlock, Carmina, Huldra, and Thor checked into the hotel Flatwoods. Huldra insisted on two rooms; Carmina was happy to oblige, though the rooms would be next to each other.

Before they departed for their rooms for some rest and cold pizza, they picked up from a local restaurant.

"Okay, Sherlock, get some rest tomorrow, we have some trekking to do through the woods. Don't let Huldra here keep you up."

"I can always keep him up."

Huldra winked at Carmina, who rolled her eyes.

"Do not worry, plenty of time to rest and feel refreshed for tomorrow, Carmina. Though I think Laney was not being candid with us."

Sherlock could not get a good read on Laney; he attributed his lack of awareness to being tired from the car ride.

"Maybe, but if she knows something about these missing people, why wouldn't she tell the cops?"

Huldra asked with genuine interest.

"Not sure, but I do know that Brian fellow was irate; he also seemed like a bully. Plus, he insulted Thor. So, he is already on my shit list."

Thor looked up at Sherlock, wagging his tail.

"We will meet here tomorrow at 9 a.m. sharp."

Carmina did not want any of the cold pizza; she went into her room, letting the metal door shut behind her.

Huldra, Sherlock, and their furry companion entered their room.

Once they were inside, they couldn't care less about the food; they wanted to hop into bed and let their bodies release whatever pent-up energy remained from the day.

"Sherlock, are you hungry?"

Sherlock had tossed the pizza box onto the small table in the room by the window.

"I am, but not for pizza."

He smiled at her. She leaned down and released Thor's collar. He went merrily to explore the room.

Sherlock drew the curtains closed.

Huldra removed her clothes as Sherlock watched her intently.

She tossed the pizza box onto the floor, climbed up to the table, and sat there with her legs spread open.

"Time for you to have a meal."

She said as she leaned her head back, looking at the ceiling while holding her torso up with her hands behind her.

Sherlock removed his coat, hat, vest, and necktie.

He sat on a chair from the table set, pulling it as close as possible to Huldra. He grabbed her legs, lifted them in the air, and began slowly licking her pussy. Her hands gripped the table as she leaned back onto it.

Huldra moaned so loud that Carmina could hear her in the next room, prompting the annoyed driver to bang on the wall.

"Can you two please keep it down?!"

They didn't even hear her complaint over the sound of the slurping Sherlock was doing. He placed her clit in his mouth and began slowly sucking it towards him, in and out. The motion made Huldra's entire pussy quake.

"Don't stop doing that, that feels so good."

Huldra was able to get the words out between breaths. Her encouragement made Sherlock continue that motion.

She reached over her chest with her hands, squeezing her tits as Sherlock licked her to her heart's content.

Sherlock pulled back, stood up, unbuckled his pants, kicked off his shoes one foot at a time, then pulled his pants and boxers down and off.

Huldra raised her head a little to see Sherlock's cock. It was not as pale as the rest of him. It had a tanned look to it; his cock head was thick. She could see the veins protruding from the top. She saw it the night before, but this time she took in more detail of him.

Sherlock, still standing up, went to the edge of the table where Huldra was impatiently waiting.

He grabbed his cock, slowly rubbing it on her clit, moving it up and down within her pussy lips. Teasing her before he entered her soft flower.

Slowly, Sherlock slid his shaft into Huldra, holding her legs up in the air while he did. He continued holding her as he thrusted into her slowly. He would back his cock out just enough before the head came out of her, then he would slowly push it back in.

Though he loved the spontaneous, downright fucking. He enjoyed taking his time, pleasing his partner. Sherlock derived his pleasure from Huldra receiving hers.

He looked down at her, admiring her body.

"Huldra, you look so fucking sexy."

She smiled as her eyes closed, taking in as much of Sherlock as he was willing to give. His cock didn't make her feel stretched; it made her feel full, from the inside out.

Sherlock, still thrusting methodically into her, grabbed and slid his hands from holding up her ankles to holding her legs up by her feet, which were bigger than his hands, but only by a small amount.

He leaned his head down, biting her ankle while still filling her with his cock.

"You fuck me so good, Sherlock."

He could feel her legs begin to shake, her thighs becoming firmer, her toes curling.

"Don't stop, Sherlock, please don't stop."

By her body's reaction, he knew she was close to climaxing. He was close too.

Huldra screamed in ecstasy as her pussy tightened around his cock.

"I'm cumming!"

That phrase, her sexy body, and great pussy would not allow Sherlock to last any longer. It seems that Huldra must have felt Sherlock was close to cumming, she begged him to stay inside her.

"Don't pull away, stay inside."

He obeyed her, his cum filled her as they both were moaning, their bodies moist, melting, and dripping into each other.

Once Sherlock unloaded every drop into Huldra, he sat down in the chair behind his legs.

He reached down to the floor to locate his vest pocket, pulled out one of his cannabis cigarettes, and his lighter. He lit his cannabis cigarette, took two puffs, then reached over to Huldra, who was still catching her breath on her back on top of the hotel room table.

Huldra grabbed the cigarette, took a couple of puffs, and exhaled.

She giggled, sat up to look at Sherlock.

"Don't worry, baby, I'll suck your cock someday."

She said with a devilish smile.

They both laughed, now they could truly relax before their venture the next morning.

Chapter 32

That night, Laney walked to her backyard, looking up at the night sky. The magnetism in her chest began to pull; she knew it meant Vald was nearby.

The night sky's stars were interrupted by a flash of a winged creature zooming past. She could hear the large flaps of his enormous wings breaking the silence.

He landed in her yard, and the chain around his neck rattled as he landed.

"My queen."

He took a few steps closer to Laney.

"Mothy, I am so glad to see you."

She embraced Vlad, slipping her arms around his waist, resting her head on his chest.

"I told my aunt about you. I told her about us."

Mothman's glowing red eyes stared at her.

"I trust your judgement, Laney."

"Tomorrow, I must take some people to the woods, as they are investigating the people who have disappeared. You must not be around when I do. They are looking for you; word has gotten out about a winged creature in the forest. The townspeople are scared."

"Are you scared, Laney?"

His voice was heavy; it turned her on, but she tried not to think about that now.

"I haven't been scared of anything since I met you, Vlad, other than myself."

"Tomorrow, my aunt will go with me to show these investigators the area where those dipshits and I were. She will sway them away from the sights. Though one of them is a famous detective, he will be harder to distract. Once they have looked around for a while, finding nothing, they will figure it is a moot point and will leave."

"What about tonight?"

Laney looked at Mothman with confusion on her face.

"What about tonight, Vlad?"

"I need more of you, my queen, please command me."

His voice was begging for his master to tell her slave what to do. Either way, it had been a stressful day, the best way for her to relax in her mind was to fuck her Mothman.

"Follow me."

She said it with confidence as he walked behind her until they reached the door of the metal shed, where she found his chain collar. He had to bring his wings closed to enter the small doorway.

Laney slid open the rusted shed door, walking into the darkness of it.

The shed had random hardware stuff inside, the typical objects one keeps addressing maintenance around their house. There was a shelf with old paint cans, a wall with a few tools hanging from a pegboard, and a solid wood workbench with a few random spray cans and jars of screws.

Laney reached over and turned on a kerosene lantern, illuminating the shed.

The orange glow shows their faces in fluttering light.

Laney took off the straps over her shoulders of the black dress she was wearing, letting it fall carelessly to the floor.

She leaned over the workbench, spreading her legs enough to give Mothman space to get under her.

She placed her hand flat on the workbench table, her breasts hanging down right outside the edge.

"Command me, master, I will do whatever my queen says."

Laney turned her head back, looking at Mothman.

"Crawl over to me and eat my ass, slave."

Mothman kneeled, fighting hard for his wings not to expand in excitement. He crawled on his claw-like hands and knees to her; she could hear his claws scraping the floor of the shed.

Vlad proceeded to place his claws on Laney's ass cheeks, spreading them apart, allowing her asshole to come into his full view.

Laney moaned at the anticipation of the forbidden gesture of Mothman's tongue in her ass.

Laney could feel the forked tongue crossing over the back of her thigh, down to her pussy, just enough to brush her clit. Then he moved his tongue to her ass as she had commanded.

His tongue licked around her asshole softly, caressing every wrinkle. He slid his tongue inside her asshole.

"Fuck me with your tongue, slave."

She moaned as the forked tongue continued its descent into her.

Never had she felt anything like this; her pussy was wet, dripping from the pleasure of his tongue. His cock in her ass felt good once she got used to it, but this was a different sensation; his tongue was gentle, yet powerful.

She was grasping for anything she could grab or get a hold of; she placed her hand around one of the jars of screws, holding it tight while his tongue explored her asshole.

His claws dug into her ass cheeks to keep them spread open. While his tongue was in her, she began sliding back on it, taking control, her ass moved towards his face, then away from it.

"Devour me, slave." She commanded.

The words left her mouth in a huff, and Vlad's eyes grew brighter red. Tasting her from inside her ass brought him closer to her, to every orifice she had that he wanted to explore.

His cock had already expanded out; he was turned on. Fucking her with his tongue was pleasing him just as it was bringing her pleasure.

Laney threw the jar she was holding off the table, causing it to shatter on the floor. She did not care; all she cared about now was getting her ass eaten.

Mothman released her ass cheeks; they closed around his tongue, while his master continued to move back and forth on his forked tongue. Just as the tip would reach the edge of her asshole, she could feel both parts go into her, rubbing against the top of her asshole and the bottom.

"That's a good slave, keep that tongue right there."

"Yes, my queen."

✳✳✳

"My queen's ass tastes so good. The way her body grips my tongue to slide on, I can feel every inch of her folds going towards my mouth."

Mothman would catch glimpses of her tits that were hanging down, slapping her stomach back and forth. They were plump, heavy, and sagged on her chest in a way that drove him wild.

Then, Laney lifted one of her legs, placing her foot on the edge of the table, opening her asshole even further.

"You are exquisite, my master."

Laney could hear the chain slapping against his broad chest.

"Did master tell you to speak?" She asserted through heavy breaths.

"No, my queen."

Mothman grabbed the ankle of her leg that was on the floor, pushed his tongue even deeper into Laney's ass, and she moaned to his delight. Pleasing his queen is all he cares about.

"She is delicious, every inch, every fold."

Laney kept knocking things off the workbench table; the noises coming from the shed of shattering glass, moans, and metal tools hitting the wall alerted her aunt. Her aunt did not go outside. Laney told her she would be with the monster that night. Her aunt could see a glow of light coming from the bottom of the shed. She smiled, went to the kitchen, poured a glass of wine for herself, then turned the radio on loud enough to muddle the sound from the outside somewhat.

Her leg was beginning to shake from being on one leg for so long, with the other propped up. Though she was close to cumming and was not about to lose this anal orgasm, even if it did mean her leg would give out.

"Almost there, slave, keep licking deeper."

He did not respond to her; she made it clear that he was to speak when his queen told him to.

"I'm about to cum!"

She screamed, then her pussy began to squirt, making her legs shake, causing her to fall back on top of Mothman, causing him to fall backwards. Now she was on him, ass in his face, cock in hers. This was a happy accident; he began drinking her nectar that was squirting on his face. She looked at his two-headed erect cock. She was on top of him in a sixty-nine position. She began sucking on his cock head, one at a time, then back and forth between both while she stroked his shaft.

"I need her nectar, it is delicious."

Laney licked around his cockheads, flicking her tongue in and out like a snake as she went around the brim of each. She bit the top of one head.

"Do you like that slave?"

She asked as he muffled out an answer through a face full of pussy.

She bit him down his shaft until her lips reached the feather grouping. She placed her hand on the group of feathers, and under it, she could feel his testicles. It felt interesting to her, not wrinkled as she expected; it was relatively smooth yet firm.

Laney licked Mothman's cock from the base to the end, where his cock split into two heads.

Vlad was about to burst, but he did not say anything to Laney, too focused on eating her to speak.

As she was licking his shaft down again, his cock erupted. First one head shot out a load of cum, followed by the second head. The first shot went somewhere. Laney couldn't see. The second went out and back down, glazing her hand over while she held his cock. She removed her

hand from him, licked her palm, and slowly stood up.

She was gathering strength in her leg muscles again as they began to twitch.

"Did I tell you to cum, Mothy?"

She asked with some discontent in her voice.

"I'm sorry, my mistress, I could not help it.

Laney smiled.

"Your master isn't complaining. Next time, you cum when I tell you to, got it?"

Mothman rolled to one side, lifted himself, kneeling at the feet of his naked master.

Laney placed her arms around his shoulders, kissed his forehead, and embraced him.

"Don't ever leave me, Vlad."

"I will never leave you, my queen."

Chapter 33

Sherlock, Huldra, Carmina, and Thor got up early to meet Officer Owens at the scene where Bubba Chance's car was found. This was arranged earlier by Carmina; they told Laney nothing about this early-morning meeting on purpose.

Bubba Chance's car was still considered an active crime scene from where the Mothman had left it.

Sherlock looked around the car, and he peeked his head inside the vehicle, taking a brief look.

"Tell me, Officer Owens, do you have a theory about what might have happened to Mr. Chance?"

"Well, he liked to drink. We think he got drunk after taking his employee home, drove off the road, and wandered into the woods. Hell, he may still be in a drunken heap somewhere in the woods."

"Interesting assessment, Officer Owens."

The officer smiled, puffed out his chest, and was proud of himself.

"Well, thank you, Mr. Holmes."

"I said it was interesting, I never said it was correct."

Sherlock stated, much to the officer's aggravation.

"Well, you have a better explanation?"

The officer was taken down a few pegs with Sherlock's comment.

Sherlock reached into his jacket pocket, pulled out a cigar that already had the end cut off. He pulled out his lighter from his pants pocket and lit his cigar while everyone stared at him.

His patience could be infuriating sometimes.

"Hey, Mr. Holmes, you can't smoke that here; this is a crime scene!"

"Where would you prefer me to smoke it?"

Before Officer Owens could answer, Sherlock began speaking.

"Judging by the grass behind the car, there are no tire marks on the grass that show this vehicle came off the road. Furthermore, the front hood has been dented in two spots, as if by two powerful hands. Simply put, this car was pushed to this spot. Whatever went awry, happened somewhere else."

"Huldra, tell me, what kind of cryptid could do this sort of thing?"

Huldra was on the spot; the whole purpose of her coming along was not to fuck Sherlock, though that was indeed a bonus. She was brought along because she knew cryptids, no more than Carmina, but Carmina had to pretend that she knew very little about them.

"Not all cryptids come from the woods, Sherlock. Though this one surely did, something substantial that can push a car through brush, and can fly? The list isn't as long as you think."

"There are cryptids that can shape shift. Unless what we have is a cross cryptid."

Huldra stated with some skepticism.

Carmina looked over at Huldra; if looks could kill, she would be dead.

"What is a cross cryptid?"

Sherlock asked his petite lover.

"It's a cross between one creature that becomes a cryptid, that is nonhuman."

Sherlock stared at Huldra blankly.

"For example, Sherlock, a werewolf that becomes a night crawler or a vampire that becomes a lizard man."

"Very interesting, Huldra. So, you believe a cross cryptid may have done this?"

"I'm not sure, Sherlock, but I know whatever did this could not have been human."

She was confident in her answer.

"Have you recovered his body, Officer Owens?"

Sherlock wanted to see how much the police department believed Bubba Chance was alive.

"No, we haven't. I am sure we will find him soon."

The arrogance in the officer's voice was thick.

"Unlikely, anyone or anything that went through the trouble of placing this vehicle here would not have left much of a body to recover if there was one."

"What do you mean, Holmes?"

Carmina answered the officer on Sherlock's behalf.

"He means, Bubba Chance is dead. I agree with his assessment."

"Officer Owens, have you traced the area back into the woods?"

"Well, no, not really, we sent in a few officers to search for him."

The officer hesitated to answer, knowing that the most likely outcome was that Sherlock would call him out for being shortsighted in his police work.

Sherlock walked away before Owens could answer. The detective walked from the hood of the vehicle into the dense woods it faced. Carmina followed behind him, and Huldra stayed back with Officer Owens, watching over Thor.

Sherlock reached a landing spot: a clearing surrounded by trees. The tire marks from there were visible. He nodded his head, admitting to himself that he was right about the car being placed where it was. At some point, the vehicle was in this location.

Sherlock paced the area. Carmina alerted him to significant paw marks on the ground near where the tire marks on the grass were made.

"Sherlock, look at this. A wolf print, larger than an average-sized dog."

Sherlock kneeled, and he placed his finger on the paw indentation.

"Whatever kind of wolf this was, it was heavy. Its weight created a small depth with its print on the soil, suggesting something that must weigh a minimum of one hundred kilos."

Sherlock then saw a significant clue. A half-talon print on the ground was large and gnarly looking. He could see the prints leading toward the tire track marks.

"The creature pushed this vehicle away. Maybe it was invading its territory, I am not certain, but whatever got Bubba Chance was not human."

"Come, Carmina, let us head back to town. We must meet with Laney; she must take us to the spot she came to."

"What remains were left, surely were picked apart by the crows or vultures."

Sherlock found some evidence of an attack, but not enough yet to reach a solid conclusion about what happened to the restaurant owner.

Chapter 34

When the detective arrived with his team at Laney's house, she was already waiting outside with her Aunt Monica.

As they approached, Sherlock rolled down the passenger side window.

"Sherlock, meet my Aunt Monica. She just got her car back; she took a taxi this morning and picked it up from where I worked."

"Pleasure to meet you. Very well, we will follow your lead. We just came from close to that area, I believe. Police officers were investigating a car that belonged to your boss."

Laney and her aunt stood silent for a moment. Sherlock measured this deliberate silence as further evidence that he knew Laney was hiding something.

"Let's go, we will follow your car."

Carmina was eager to get this show on the road.

Once Monica backed the car out of the driveway, they were on their way to the location Laney promised to take them to. What Sherlock did not realize was that they were being followed.

****

By the time they arrived, the police presence was gone. Sherlock noted the proximity of where Laney took them in relation to the location where Bubba Chance's vehicle was found.

They all arrived at the clearing and got out of the car. This location was, in fact, where she took the three college boys that night—again, mixing truth with lies.

"This is where we came. I got out of the car, went into the woods from here, and Matt followed me."

"Why did he follow you? What did he think he was going to get?"

Sherlock knew the answer, but thought Laney should be specific in case she was lying and would forget details.

"He thought I was going to suck his dick, okay?"

Sherlock looked over at Huldra. She gave him the middle finger, and he returned his attention to Laney.

He scanned the ground, finding remnants of dried blood everywhere.

"How did you get home?"

Sherlock asked point-blank.

"What?" She was caught off guard. Of all the things she had an answer for, being flown by Mothman home was not one of them.

She hesitated to answer; she threw out a desperate lie.

"My friend Jordie picked me up."

"Nonsense, my dear, she did not know you were out here." Sherlock moved closer to Laney. Laney felt the magnetism in her chest again, which meant her monster was nearby.

"How did you get home?"

No answer came, then the silence was broken by someone shouting.

"Answer him bitch!"

From the woods emerged Brian, holding a shotgun, facing Laney. He was the one tailing them in his car.

Sherlock reached for his revolver slowly, while the attention was not on him.

"Don't you point that gun at my niece, you asshole!"

Monica screamed at Brian.

"Tell them what you did to Matt and Kirk. I know you did something."

Carmina had every bit of ability to end this in an instant. She could not, though; she had to keep her cover story intact by being a research librarian, which was far too important for the greater good.

Huldra was angry, and Thor growled at the human whom he used as a piss pole the day before.

Brian chambered the shotgun; he lifted the barrel, then came a loud thud.

Mothman landed in front of Laney, making Brian lose his balance, though he did not fall.

Mothman flashed his fierce fangs, he growled like the savage creature he was, and Brian squeezed off a shot.

Laney pushed Vlad out of the way with all her strength. The bullet struck her in the chest as she flew backwards, hitting the ground.

Sherlock drew his revolver, firing three shots in the direction of Brian, hitting him with two bullets, one in the elbow, the other in the shoulder. Brian dropped the shotgun and started bleeding profusely. He grabbed his shoulders while falling to his knees.

"NO! My Queen!" Mothman flew to Laney's side.

He placed his claw-hands on the side of her face. For a moment, his face returned to human form. He kissed Laney gently on the forehead. Staring down at her, while her chest bled with a massive hole in it.

Then his face reverted to that of the creature with bulging, red, glowing eyes, massive wings, and a shit ton of strength.

He flew in great haste, grabbing Brian by the neck.

Carmina, Sherlock, Huldra, and Thor looked on with shock; they had no idea what Mothman was about to do to Brian.

"You killed my queen, now you die!"

Mothman's voice was hot with rage.

Brian peed himself out of fear.

"Pathetic, weak human."

Suddenly, a noise caught their attention: the sound of loud leather wings flapping. They all turned to find Laney standing up, with wings coming out of her back, fangs protruding through her mouth. Her eyes glowed white, giving her a ghostly appearance, the wound on her chest gone, though her clothes still sported the blood that came out of her.

Her wings had a purple hue, her hands still human, but her forearms now had small grayish feathers protruding from her skin.

Her black dress was shredded in parts; the gunshot created an opening exposing some of her voluptuous breasts. Laney's bare feet were floating just above the ground.

Laney's aunt smiled.

The Goth Moth was now born.

Carmina huffed the word "shit" under her breath.

Sherlock was not sure who to point the revolver at, and Huldra was turned on by Sherlock firing the shot.

"Leave him my slave; he is mine to dismember."

Laney hissed in a ghostly voice.

Mothman turned and smiled; his queen was floating a foot above the forest floor, flowing towards him. They kissed and embraced as their wings flapped. Mothman and his master, not even death could separate them.

The devilish Laney looked blankly at Brian. She began to laugh, and he began to cry.

Mothman was still holding Brian by his neck.

Laney floated behind Brian. She reached her clawed hand into his back, and his eyes began to fill with blood. From his back, she pulled out his beating heart, taking an enormous bite out of it. She then offered it to her lover.

Vlad took a bite of the heart, then dropped the body of Brian that he was still holding.

Mothman and Laney looked back at the mostly humans that were behind him.

Mothman looked at Carmina with kind eyes.

"Carmina? Why are you here?"

Sherlock looked at Carmina in amazement.

"Is it possible you literally know everyone and every creature in this place?"

Carmina ignored Sherlock's question.

"I thought it was you, Vlad. I see we must incorporate a new member into La Lechuza.

"Welcome, Laney."

Carmina turned to Monica.

"Thank you for calling our associate. I received your message."

"Of course, Carmina, I knew you would want to know that my niece found a cryptid."

Huldra looked up at Sherlock.

"Care to explain, lover?"

"It seems that Laney is in love with this moth fellow. This Brian moron, who is now dead, asserted that he had a sexual relationship with Laney. He lied to his friends. Brian told his friends that she was an easy fuck. When his friends took Laney to the woods, they encountered Mothman. Judging by the size of his fangs, I would say he may initially have hailed from Romania. That accent, I would not forget. I met him in human form in a train station on my way to Georgia."

"I assume Bubba Chance was your doing, Vlad?"

"It was, though we both know that is not what you will say when anyone asks."

"Surely not, your secret is safe with me, after all, I am getting used to keeping secrets for monsters."

"When we first met Laney, I noticed bite marks on both sides of her neck. It was clear to me that whatever made those marks must have had long fangs. Being on both sides of her neck told me she moved her head from one side to the other to be bitten; she welcomed it."

Laney walked her full figure over to where her aunt was, retracting her wings.

"Tia, you can always find me; we are connected. I will always be in the woods of Point Pleasant, West Virginia, with my love. But I will visit you often, you still owe me more details about my mom, La Llorona (Yo-Ro-Na), thank you for taking care of me."

Sherlock heard the name Selma used; he just figured out that his ghostly sexual encounter on the ship that took him to the States was Laney's mother. He remained silent, said nothing; it was yet another secret he would have to pocket.

"It was nice meeting you again, Sherlock. Carmina, could you take care of the rest of this? Laney and I have a date tonight on a bridge.

"Of course, very romantic, Vlad."

Carmina reassured him.

With that, Laney and Vlad flew off together, claw in claw hand, wings side by side, master and slave.

Chapter 35

Sherlock, his newly acquired lover, Carmina, and Thor all sat around a dinner table thinking of what their next plan should be. The restaurant was empty, so they did not give Thor much trouble for coming inside.

"That was quite the mystery, Sherlock."

"Yes, it was Huldra, though a few things remain open-ended."

"For example?" She asked with curiosity while raising a cream-colored ceramic mug to her lips, taking a sip of coffee.

"It seems Carmina here is more connected to things than I thought. La Lechuza organization, which I am very curious about, is one of those things she is connected to. You warned me she was a Death Dealer; all I know is she has secrets."

Carmina stared across the table at both Sherlock and Huldra.

"We all have our secrets, Sherlock. The one thing I will tell you is I am part of an organization that helps protect creatures like Vlad and Skookum. To us, they aren't Mothman or Bigfoot; they are part of our world."

Sherlock nodded, looked down at Thor, reached over and petted him, while slipping Thor a slice of bacon.

"So now what do we do?"

Huldra asked, clearly giving no indication she was going to leave their side anytime soon.

"Elementary, my dear Huldra, we research as a team our next case. Carmina here will be a great resource. Though in the future, Carmina, please tell me which case to investigate as opposed to leading me to the monster I am supposed to find."

"You weren't supposed to find this one, but yes, I get your point. Just remember, Sherlock, there is a difference between omitting and lying."

"Noted, whatever happened to that Jerry fellow?"

Sherlock asked, forgetting the fate of the witness.

"Let's just say he was part of my job as a Death Dealer. He isn't around anymore. Before you ask, no, you cannot investigate his disappearance."

"Shall we travel to Twain, Georgia, then?"

Huldra asked patiently.

"So does that mean you are coming with us, Huldra, or are we dropping you off back in Roanoke?"

Huldra looked at Sherlock as if the question was utterly absurd.

"Depends, you want that blowjob or not?"

Sherlock looked at Carmina for approval.

"Huldra will be traveling with us."

Sherlock stated with glee. Carmina rolled her eyes.

"How about this? We find the next case from here. Then we decide where to go, and we can work out of the hotel room for now. I know the owner, we can stay as long as we like."

Carmina's suggestion seemed to be agreeable to everyone at the table.

"Very well, it is settled, our next monster case we will find it from here. Though I do wonder how Watson is doing."

"He is fine; he happens to be a new associate of the organization."

Carmina said, then she shot a look at Sherlock, which meant not asking further questions.

"Excellent."

Sherlock felt confident enough that if this organization could protect monsters, it could surely protect Watson. Though Sherlock did not know, his dear friend and partner is the new Plague Doctor working for the La Lechuza organization.

Epilogue

Carmen, the mother of Carmina, was walking across the Pine Barrens of the New Jersey woods. Her leather black knee-high boots added to her strut.

She approached a dark figure who was holding a cane, wearing a top hat, standing over a bloody corpse.

He heard her footsteps and turned around.

"Well, Aaron, it seems like you have made yourself right at home."

The figure spun around to see a sultry witch standing behind him. He was fearful; this was the leader of the organization he was ousted from. He feared her, knowing what she was capable of.

"Carmen, what are you doing here?"

She instantly picked up on the nervousness of his voice.

"You did not actually think we would forget the damage you did in London, Aaron, did you?"

"Well, I assume that because you allowed me to leave the country…"

Carmen interrupted him with a wave of his hand.

"There is no world where La Lechuza organization would allow you to harm innocent people with no repercussions. They called you the London Ripper. You got that Jack fool to do part of your bidding, while he sits in the Tower of London, you are here, still ripping people to shreds in the pine woods of New Jersey. I am afraid that time is over."

Aaron took a step back. He was covered in blood from his latest victim. Whatever horrible act he just committed could not compare to the terrible fate he was about to face.

"You like being a devil, don't you, Aaron? No worries, I will make you the devil you want to be."

Carmen moved back. She chanted under her breath, rubbing both of her fingers together.

Suddenly, Aaron dropped to the floor in pain. He screamed as his face elongated, his hands and feet turning into hooves. His clothes were disintegrating in the heat of his body; the agony of having his body morphed was excruciating.

Carmen kept chanting, his body turning into that of a goat horse, and he grew a tail shaped like a devil's arrow at the end of it.

Then he sprouted wings, and they ripped up out of the back of his hide.

He was confused, in pain, and scared.

Carmen had a sinister smile.

"I curse you to this form, for as long as your hooves trample this soil, you are affixed to these woods. From this moment on, you will be known as the Jersey Devil."

About the Author

N.S. Thorngrave is a master of weaving mystery, desire, and the macabre into stories that linger long after the final page. His work fuses the thrill of gothic suspense with the seductive pull of erotica, creating a reading experience that is as chilling as it is intoxicating.

Born and raised in Miami, Florida, Thorngrave now writes from the mist-laden mountains of Northern Georgia, where the surrounding forests fuel his fascination with cryptids, secrets, and the shadows that haunt the human heart. With every tale, he invites readers into worlds where danger and passion entwine— stories crafted to both intrigue the mind and ignite the senses.